Paper Thin

The Lip Gloss Chronicles

SHELIA M. GOSS

URBAN Renaissance

www.urbanbooks.net

Urban Books, LLC
1199 Straight Path
West Babylon, NY 11704

ISBN-13: 978-1-60162-204-4
ISBN-10: 1-60162-204-X

First Printing February 2010
Printed in the United States of America

10 9 8 7 6 5 4 3 2 1

Distributed by Kensington Publishing Corp.
Submit Wholesale Orders to:
Kensington Publishing Corp.
C/O Penguin Group (USA) Inc.
Attention: Order Processing
405 Murray Hill Parkway
East Rutherford, NJ 07073-2316
Phone: 1-800-526-0275
Fax: 1-800-227-9604

ACKNOWLEDGMENTS

I thank God for allowing me to do this one more time. I appreciate all of the support my readers have given me from book one in the Lip Gloss Chronicles series until now—thank you!

Exie Goss—my mom and dad (Lloyd Goss: 1947-1996) helped mold me into the avid reader and writer that I am today. I will always be grateful for their guidance that has opened up a door of endless possibilities.

Markessia Gholston and Ariel Washington: My talented younger cousins. Never lose your enthusiasm for the written word. Thank you for sharing your work with me. Donnisha Burnham: Stay focused and keep your eye on the prize. I love you all.

Kaelen Barclay (Carla's daughter)—thanks again for taking the time out to read The Lip Gloss Chronicles during its early stages and providing feedback. I hope I've been able to portray Britney, Jasmine and Sierra in a way that will make them unforgettable.

Maxine Thompson (my agent) and Carl Weber (my publisher)—thank you both for believing in my vision for The Lip Gloss Chronicles.

Brenda, Natalie, Kevin and the rest of the Urban Books and Kensington Books family—thank you for adding your magic touch.

To the librarians, teachers, book clubs, webmasters and readers—thank you again for reading and sharing the news of The Lip Gloss Chronicles. I would like to thank the librarians of the Shreve Memorial Library for allowing me to participate in the summer reading program & Teen Read Week. The teenagers inspired me and I hope to be able to participate again in the future.

Last, but not least, I want to dedicate another book to John, DeAngelo, Cameron, Jerricka (my little diva), Jasmine (my best little friend), Ellen (mini-me) and Justin. You are our future. I pray that God guide and protect you during your childhood years. Know that your auntie and/or older cousin love you all. I've said this before, but it's worth repeating: *If you can dream it, you can be it.*

Shelia M. Goss

~ 1 ~
The Secret

"Sierra, don't tell Jorge," Maria Sanchez said to me, as I helped her sneak shopping bags into the house. The way my stepmother shopped, you could not tell we were in a recession.

If my dad found out, he would be upset. He sat the whole family down earlier this year to let us know that business was slow so we all needed to buckle down to ride out the storm. We used to have a live-in maid, but now she only comes over three times a week. My dad, a prominent Dallas real estate developer, had received many awards over the years. He was often compared to Donald Trump because whatever he touched seemed to turn to gold.

Zion and my dad were busy in the den playing a video game. This gave my stepmother and me time to put her things away. I helped her remove tags clothes as she hung them up in her closet. After what seemed like hours but was only minutes, I said, "Mom, I think I'll take a nap. All of this shopping has worn me out."

"We're about through here anyway. Dinner will be ready in about an hour," she responded. "I'm trying to make sure we eat before six. We don't want all of our hard work this past summer to go to waste do we?"

I loved Maria as if she was my own mom, but her constant obsession with my weight had gotten on my nerves. She was good at keeping secrets. My dad had no idea that our week long excursions over the summer were really weight loss retreats that she insisted she and I attend. Maria's battle with the bulge was rubbing off on me.

It was times like these that I missed Vanessa, my real mom. I was real young when she died in a car crash. My memories of her sometimes seemed vivid and strong. Then there were times that I could barely remember her. Those are the times when I would get depressed. My BFFs (Best Friends Forever),

Britney Franklin and Jasmine McNeil, usually helped get me out of my funk.

I threw myself across my bed and closed my eyes. Sleep evaded me. I fumbled with my Blackberry and called Britney. "Hey chica," I said, when she answered.

"Do you want a baby brother or sister?" Britney asked, as I heard the twins crying in the background.

"Nope. My little brother is enough."

"Precious hit Teddy Junior because he was taking up too much of my attention. Now they are both crying," she stated. It sounded like the babies were right in the phone as loud as they were.

"Call me back later. When things settle down," I said.

"No, I can talk. I just buzzed their nanny. She'll be here any minute."

"Is Jas back?" I asked.

"She got back last night. She said she was going to text you."

"She did, but she didn't mention she was back."

"I can't wait to see you guys. It seems like these last two months had us all going in different directions," Britney said. I no longer heard the twins in the background.

"At least you guys went on real vacations. I was forced to go on these retreats with my mom."

"I've never been to Albuquerque or the Poconos," Britney said.

"It may have been fun if I wasn't starving. We didn't eat anything but green vegetables and maybe a small piece of meat each time. And the long hikes. You ought to see my leg muscles. I should be fit to run a marathon."

Britney laughed. "Girl, well you should be kicking up your heels during dance rehearsal next week."

"I can't wait. I'm hoping we get to perform more this year."

"Me too. I've been practicing some moves. You ought to come over tomorrow so I can show you."

"I don't know. I think my mom wants me to spend quality time with her and the family tomorrow. I'll let you know."

Britney's line clicked. "Three-way Jas. That's her on my other line."

A few seconds later, Jasmine was on the line. "Did y'all miss me?" Jasmine asked.

"No," Britney and I said in unison.

"You both will be changing your tune when you see the gifts I brought back for you."

I sat up in bed while thumbing through a fashion magazine. I said, "I promise to be nice." I paused and then said, "For a minute anyway."

We all burst out laughing.

Britney placed us on hold to talk to Marcus. Jasmine said, "I thought her and Marcus were through."

"They're just friends," I said, in her defense.

"She knows he still likes her so I don't know why she keeps stringing him along."

"I heard that," Britney said, alerting us she was back on the line.

"Well you are. Marcus is not just trying to be your friend. He wants more. You know it and we know it."

Jasmine and I didn't always agree on everything but I did agree with her about Marcus' intentions with Britney. Britney and Marcus were boyfriend and girlfriend for a few months but because of Marcus' cousin, Dylan Johnson or DJ as we called him, their relationship fizzled. Just the thought of DJ, my worst nightmare, made my skin crawl. I thought I was in love with him. He would have taken advantage of my feelings if my friends hadn't intervened.

I heard my name called a few times snapping me out of my bad memory of DJ. "Bri, spill the beans.

Are you and Marcus back together or what?" I asked.

"We are just friends. How many times do I have to tell you guys that," Britney said, sounding frustrated.

"Enough about Bri. I met the cutest guy on the cruise ship. He lives in Los Angeles. Get this. He has relatives in Shreveport so when he comes down to visit, we'll be hooking up," Jasmine said. She loved being the center of attention. It was clear that this past summer didn't change her in that aspect.

We continued to listen to Jasmine tell us about her summer vacation. It had been two months since we had seen each other because of our family summer schedules. My two BFFs would be in for a surprise when they saw me—twenty-five pounds less of me. It's not like I was keeping a secret, but after Jasmine taunted me last year about my weight gain I didn't feel comfortable talking to them about my size.

Jasmine and Britney were naturally thin. Me, I had to work hard at maintaining an average weight. My birth mom was what folks called big-boned. I inherited it from not only her but my dad's side of the family. My cousins said that I shouldn't try to lose weight because guys loved a girl with a big butt. According to them, when I get older I will appreciate having the bigger booty.

I don't know about that, but I do know my weight at the time was one hundred and seventy pounds and it had me stressing. It was more than likely the reason I became DJ's victim. I needed to work on more than my weight; I needed to work on my attitude and let bygones be bygones. Dealing with DJ and almost losing my friends because of him, led to an unforgettable freshman year. I was anxious to see what challenges I would face my sophomore year at one hundred and forty-five pounds.

~ 2 ~
Back to School

It didn't take me long to get dressed for the first day of school. My mom had family activities planned for us so I didn't get a chance to hang out with Britney or Jasmine before now. As I admired myself in the mirror, it felt good to be wearing my new school uniforms. They were two sizes smaller than what they were last year. I ran my hair through my freshly permed hair one last time, before leaving to join my mom in the car.

The trip to Plano High wasn't like my freshman year. This year I had more confidence. I felt more secure. I felt like with my new slimmer look I was going to have a great year. My biggest challenge would be maintaining my perfect grade point average. New teachers and harder classes awaited me.

As we pulled up in the driveway of Plano High School, I put on watermelon lip gloss. "One reason you get hungry is because you pick those lip gloss flavors that make you think of food, dear," my mom said, as she glanced at me.

"Maria," I whined. I called her Maria instead of Mom when she got on my nerves.

"Make sure you choose salad over a greasy burger for lunch," she kept talking as I finished primping in the visor mirror.

"Yes Maria," I responded. I would eat what I felt like eating, but she didn't have to worry. I worked too hard to lose weight over the summer. I had no intentions of gaining back the weight. Besides, from what I read on the internet eating a burger every now and then wouldn't hurt. I just needed to do it in moderation.

I checked out my reflection one last time before exiting the car. I waved at my mom as she drove away. I glanced around the school campus to see if I could locate Britney or Jasmine. I noticed the scared looks of some of the new faces. I was grateful I was no longer a freshman. I put a little more bounce in my step as it seemed more guys were taking notice of me and my new look.

I decided to wait in the front of the school at what we deemed "our spot." While waiting to see if Britney or Jasmine would show up, a boy with the cutest dimples I had ever seen walked up to me and spoke. I looked around to see if maybe someone was standing behind me. Maybe he had me mistaken for someone else. *Get a grip.* I told myself. "Hi," I finally responded.

"Can you tell me where the office is?" he asked.

I looked around to see if any one of my friends were in view. No sign of them, so I couldn't let the cutie down. "I can do better than that. I can show you," I said, hoping I didn't sound too eager.

"I'm Cameron Crenshaw by the way," he said, as we walked.

I responded, "Nice to meet you." I didn't bother to tell him my name. It wasn't because I didn't want to. Cameron had me at a loss for words.

It didn't take us long to get to the office. "Who should I be thanking?" he asked, while pausing at the door.

"Sierra," I stuttered. I wanted to slap myself. *What happened to the new confident Sierra?*

"Well Sierra, I hope to see you around. Thanks

again." He winked his left eye and left me standing outside of the office.

"Sierra is that you? I told Bri, that was you," Jasmine yelled, as she and Britney walked up to me. We exchanged hugs.

Britney said, "Girl, I love the new look."

"I love your hair," I said. Over the summer Britney had cut her hair to shoulder length and died it jet black. Because of her light complexion, sometimes folks questioned her ethnic background. Both of her parents were African-American and Britney would be quick to tell anyone her heritage if they tried to question it.

Jasmine ran her hands through my now straight hair. "You got rid of all of those curls. I like it."

"Thanks," I responded.

Jasmine stood back a little as if she wanted to get a full view of me. "There's something else that's changed. I just can't put my finger on it."

I saved her the frustration of trying to figure it out. "Would it be I lost a little weight?"

"Oh, yes. That's it. Girl you look fan-tab-u-lous," Jasmine said.

Jasmine was used to being the center of attention. I could tell she felt a little left out in the compliments department since neither I nor Britney mentioned anything special about her. In my opinion, there was no need to. Jasmine's ego was bigger than both of ours combined so we didn't need to add to it.

We were instructed by one of the teachers greeting students in the hallway to meet in the general assembly area to pick up our schedules for the semester. Jasmine opened up her back pack and pulled out two gift bags. "This is for you," she said, as she handed me a cute floral gift bag.

She then handed Britney a larger gift bag. I wasn't sure if I should be jealous or not. I then recalled Maria once saying that it's not the size of the bag of a gift, but what's inside. I would have to wait to open it, because by now we were standing outside of the auditorium. I didn't want to give a faculty member any reason to confiscate anything from me, so I placed my gift in my backpack.

Jasmine looked a little disappointed. "You're not going to open them now?"

Britney said, "Girl, you know how these folks can be."

"But I wanted to see your expressions," she responded.

I said, "Pact. We promise to wait until lunch to

open them. That way if I don't like mine, you'll know it right on the spot."

Britney burst out laughing. Jasmine didn't.

Cameron walked up to me at this point. "Thanks again for earlier," he said.

"No problem," I responded. Jasmine cleared her throat a few times. I ignored her.

"See you around," he said, before walking away.

~ 3 ~

Dimples

"Who was that?" Britney asked.

"Cameron," I responded nonchalantly.

Jasmine said, "He must be new because I don't remember seeing him last year. I would have definitely remembered those dimples."

"I didn't ask." I tried to play down my attraction to Cameron. I knew he was new because if he wasn't he wouldn't have been asking me for directions on how to get to the office.

Britney said, "So we won't have a repeat of our freshman year, let's get some stuff clear."

Jasmine pretended like she had no idea what Britney was referring to. I could never forget the Dylan Johnson fiasco that caused me plenty of sleepless nights. I almost messed up my grade point average because of dealing with him and the stress it caused between me and my friends.

Jasmine asked, "Bri, you can't tell me you didn't find Cameron attractive?"

Britney responded, "I didn't say that. But it's obvious Sierra already has her eyes set on him, so there's no need for us to drool over him."

I said, "For the record, I just met him this morning."

One of the school administrators interrupted our conversation. "Young ladies you need to get in your respective lines and pick up your schedules. You can talk during your breaks."

"Yes ma'am," we responded in unison.

"Check your phones," Britney said, right before we all went to stand in different lines.

While standing in the "S" line since my last name is Sanchez, I checked the instant messenger set up on my phone. Britney sent a message to both me and Jasmine.

Britney typed, "Do you like Cameron or not?"

"I just met him, but I do think he's a hottie," I responded in our private chat room.

"She likes him," Jasmine responded. "I promise not to pursue him. I don't want Sierra to have to deal with a broken heart."

Jasmine was doing her best to get under my skin but I refused to let her. I ignored the last few instant messages and picked up my schedule from the school administrator. I was scanning my schedule when Britney and Jasmine walked up holding their schedules. We compared, and to all of our surprise we all had the same homeroom again. We were also relieved to learn that our lunch schedules were the same.

Britney and I were in dance class together. Jasmine's gym class was during the same time period but she would be taking a regular physical education course instead of dance. All of my courses were advanced courses except for geography and dance.

As we were walking to our homeroom class, we passed Cameron. I pretended not to see him. Jasmine said, "Your new friend is trying to get your attention."

I ignored her comment and without acknowledging Cameron I continued to walk to class with Britney and Jasmine. We were seated next to each other when a few minutes later, Cameron walked into the classroom. Now I knew he was a sophomore just like us. I wondered what else there was to Cameron. We waved at each other as he went to sit by Lauren Freeman. It didn't take but a second for Lauren to start flirting with him.

Britney whispered, "I see she hasn't changed one bit."

"She needs to chill," Jasmine whispered.

I said, "I don't care." Although I did care, I wasn't going to let Cameron or any other guy get under my skin. This was a new year. I would have a new attitude if it killed me.

I couldn't help but glance over in Cameron's direction while Ms. Hogan, our homeroom teacher, spoke about the rules and expectations for her geography class. I pretended to take notes but doodled my name, Cameron's name, and my name intertwined with Cameron's name in my notebook.

After homeroom class, Cameron seemed to linger around the door. "What other classes do you have?" he asked.

Before I could give him a response, Lauren had sashayed herself in front of him. His attention was now on her. I felt like I had egg on my face. For whatever reason, he must have forgotten that he and I were talking. Maybe I was too fat. Lauren was a perfect size three. I would have to starve myself to even consider going from a women's size eight to Lauren's size.

Britney said, "Girl, keep it moving. You don't want to be late for class."

I looked at Jasmine, who didn't say anything. I knew they saw what had transpired with the new kid with the dimples. I was glad they pretended not to. My new found confidence was getting shattered and it was only the first day of school.

I didn't remember I had Jasmine's gift until we were all seated across from each other at the cafeteria table during lunch. Jasmine asked, "How did you like your gifts?"

Britney responded, "I loved mine." She held out her hand and I noticed a new butterfly ring on her finger.

"Snap, I hadn't opened mine yet." I retrieved the gift back from my back pack. After disregarding the tissue paper, I saw a silver box. The box contained a gold charm bracelet adorned with charms, including one that looked like a dancer.

"Thanks Jas. This is nice," I said, as I held out my arm for her to put it on.

I twisted my arm back and forth admiring the bracelet. Jasmine was a drama queen at times and could get on my nerves, but she was one of my best friends. I knew she was someone who I could depend on through thick and thin. I would say that even if she hadn't given me the beautiful gift.

~ 4 ~

The Revelation

"How was your first day?" my mom asked, as I slipped inside the front seat of the car after school.

"It was great. I like most of my teachers. I got to hang out with Britney and Jasmine. All was good," I responded with probably more enthusiasm than she expected.

"Well I wanted to let you know that you got an invitation to Britney's birthday party."

Britney hadn't mentioned anything about having a party. I wondered why she didn't. "Really. This is the first I've heard about it," I said.

"It's a surprise so don't mention it. I didn't tell you earlier, because I know how hard it is for you girls to keep secrets from one another."

"I wouldn't have told her. I do know how to keep secrets," I said. She knew exactly what I was referring too. I had been keeping her secrets from my dad for months now.

She said, "Her party gives us an excuse to go shopping. Who knows, I might find something on sale for myself while we are shopping for you."

Did I mention my mom has a shopping addiction? I'm going to hate to be around when my dad finds out about her recent shopping excursions. Instead of heading home, we made a detour to North Park Mall. I had to practically drag my mom from the mall. We had found Britney a handbag and matching wallet from the Coach store when we first arrived at the mall. It was now after six. Not only were my feet tired but my stomach was growling. I guess she forgot her own rule about not eating after six.

"Sierra, now make sure you tell your dad we got the handbag on sale. And don't mention the other stuff. I'll keep those bags in the car."

"Yes ma'am," I responded. I really hated lying to my dad. According to my mom though, technically I wasn't lying. I was just staying out of grown folks' business. It's interesting how adults can justify the things they do. If we tried to do the same things, they would be jumping all over us for it.

Before going home, my mom pulled up into a local pizzeria parking lot. "I know this is not healthy but since you've been so good on your diet lately, I think we can splurge tonight."

While she went inside to pick up our order, I called Jasmine. "Did you know about Bri's party?"

"My mom just told me. I wish I would have known because I could have gotten her something from Paris," Jasmine responded.

"Thanks again for the perfume. My own personalized fragrance."

"They have the formula for it on file so whenever you want to re-order, just let me know and I can get you the contact info."

"My dad has us on a strict budget. I better use it sparingly because he would have a fit if I ordered some. I can only imagine how much it cost."

Jasmine said, "I used some money I had saved up."

"Girl, I guess I could dip in my savings if I ran out, but I sure hate to."

Jasmine sighed. "I sure hate how the economy is affecting everything. My dad was pissed when he had to close down most of his dealerships."

"I was watching something about how some of the car makers filed bankruptcy. I had no idea it affected your dad."

"Yes and my mom is pissed too because she's thinking her alimony and child support might be cut in half."

"I thought your dad was going to be an announcer on Monday Night football," I said.

"He is and he's assured me my lifestyle is not going to change. You know my mom is the queen of drama. She keeps listening to my aunt and reading the stuff on the gossip blogs. They keep her fired up."

"How's Brenda dealing with the divorce?" I asked.

"Now you know Brenda could care less. She's so selfish. I'm dealing with it just fine. I have two parents who spoil me and are so busy trying to outdo the other that I get benefits from them competing."

Jasmine could be a trip sometimes. I laughed when she called her sister Brenda selfish. Brenda and Jasmine were known to go at each other's throats, but despite their dysfunctional family relationship they cared about each other. Jasmine called her mom a drama queen, but as I once heard my mom say, "The apple didn't fall too far from the tree." If

Kimberly McNeil was a drama queen, Jasmine, being her daughter, held the crown as drama princess.

"There goes my mom. I'll chat with you later," I said, as my mom walked back to the car holding several pizza boxes.

"Your dad has been ringing my phone off the hook. We better get home because you know how he is when he's hungry," my mom said, as she sped out of the parking lot.

Two hours later, I was sitting in the den getting beat at a video game by my little brother Zion. I could hear my parents arguing or so it seemed because their voices got louder and louder. I wondered if my dad found out about the shopping bags. "Zion, I'm tired. You'll have to play the next game by yourself."

"You don't ever have time for me anymore," he pouted.

"You're ten years old now so you might as well get used to playing by yourself."

Little brothers could be so worrisome sometimes. I didn't mean to say those words to him, but I was in too big of a hurry to see if I could eavesdrop on my parents' conversation. I left Zion in the den playing his game as I paused outside of my parents' bedroom door.

"Maria, I found the bags, so you can stop lying about it. I'm not stupid."

"I got those things months ago."

"You're lying and you know it. The fact that you feel the need to do so says a whole lot about our relationship," my dad yelled.

"Jorge, you're making a big deal out of nothing. I'll find the receipts and take them back if it'll make you feel better."

"If you got the stuff months ago, you know most stores don't take things back after a certain amount of time."

"I promise I'll take them back. I can't remember what I did with the receipts though," she lied.

"Probably, the same thing you did with the others. Maria, I'm going to go out for a ride. While I'm out, I want you to think about how your lies have affected this family."

"But Jorge."

"But nothing. I do everything I can to provide for this family and you betray me by lying to me like I'm a fool. I've known about the shopping for awhile, but when I found out about the weight loss retreats you took my daughter on, that was the last straw for me."

Maria stuttered, "I was only looking out for

Sierra. I only did what any other mother would do."

"Sierra looks fine to me. I'm tired of this obsession you have with weight."

I could hear my mom sniffling. "I'm sorry, okay? I just don't want her to end up like me. I've always been overweight and no matter how hard I try, I can never lose these last twenty-five pounds."

I couldn't hear the rest of their conversation, because their voices got lower. I put my ear to the door, but still couldn't hear anything. My dad must have forgiven her because I never heard him leave the house.

~ 5 ~

It's Your Birthday

It was so hard keeping Britney's birthday party a secret from her. There were several times during the rest of the week that either I or Jasmine almost let it slip. Friday night was upon us. Jasmine and I had to make excuses to Britney for not being able to hang out with her over the weekend.

"I wish I could go, but Jorge and I need some alone time. Zion's with my sister and you'll be spending the night with Britney," my mom said, as she pinned up my hair.

"She's going to love the handbag and wallet. She's probably wondering why she hasn't heard from Jasmine or me to wish her a happy birthday."

"Well, have fun and remember, eat lightly."

I rolled my eyes. "I'll stop eating when I'm full." That's all I could promise.

My dad came in the room. "You look nice."

"Thanks," I said, as I admired myself in the mirror. I had on a semi-formal teal knee length dress. My dad wasn't the most affectionate person in the world, but I knew he cared about me.

"You look just like your mama. She would be so proud."

The doorbell rang. "I'll get it," Maria said. She left us to ourselves.

I sort of felt bad for my stepmother. My dad really loved my birth mom. I'm sure it was hard competing with a ghost.

Maria yelled, "Jasmine's here."

My dad reached into his pocket and handed me some money. "Times are hard right now, but not so hard that I can't make sure my daughter has her own money. Now don't use it unless it's an emergency."

I hugged him. "I won't. See you later."

A few minutes later, I was sitting in the backseat of Jasmine's mom's SUV. "You girls look so cute," Jasmine's mom said.

"Thanks Ms. Kim," I responded.

Jasmine primped in the mirror. She pulled out

several tubes of lip gloss. "Have you tried this one?" she asked me, as she turned around in the front seat before handing me a tube.

I glanced at it. "Nope. I'll have to try it sometime."

"You can have that tube. I have some more at the house," Jasmine responded.

"I'm surprised you two didn't end up spoiling Britney's surprise by telling her about the party," Ms. Kim said.

I cleared my throat. "Someone, who I will not name, almost told her yesterday when she said she wasn't going to be around this weekend because she had a party to go to."

Jasmine pushed the visor back up and leaned forward in her chair. "Good thing you were there. That's what friends are for, to have each other's back. But did you have to kick me under the table so hard?"

Ms. Kim and I laughed. Usher's latest song was playing on the CD. "Ooh, can you turn that up? That's my song," Jasmine said.

"Mine too," I added, as Ms. Kim turned up the volume. We jammed to the rest of Usher's CD all the way to the party.

We were not the first to arrive, but we did beat

the birthday girl. We were directed to enter into a private area of the arena ball. Her parents had gone all out for the party. The music was jumping and I saw several people from school that we knew. Everyone was dressed to impress. Jasmine and I slipped away from her mom.

"Girl, who invited her?" Jasmine asked.

I looked in the direction Jasmine was pointing. Lauren was the last person I wanted to see. I became really mad when I saw who she was entering the party with—Cameron.

"I guess he likes them small," Jasmine said.

"Whatever. If she's who he wants, that's his business." I would never admit to Jasmine how I felt. Yes, I was upset to see him with Lauren, but I refused to let Jasmine or anyone else know it.

"It's time," a tall man yelled to us.

Jasmine and I made our way up to the back of the room so we could be close to Britney when she entered. The lights were dimmed. The crowd became quiet. A few minutes passed and the lights were flipped on. "Surprise," we all yelled.

Britney stood shocked wearing a knee length violet evening dress. Her hair was pinned up and a diamond studded tiara was sitting on top of her head. "I can't believe this," she yelled.

Jasmine and I rushed up to her and hugged her. "I thought y'all had forgotten my birthday," Britney stammered.

Destiny Franklin, Britney's mom, said, "Now see, I told you they didn't. Now you'll listen to me."

"Thanks Mom. Thanks Dad," Britney said, as I observed her hug them both.

"Where are the twins?" I asked.

"They are with my grandparents. I thought my grandparents coming down was my birthday present and then my mom and dad insisted we go out to dinner to celebrate me turning fifteen. I had no idea they were throwing me a party."

"Well it's your birthday—so let's get this party started," Jasmine said, over the noise.

Britney seemed to be enjoying herself. I had turned fifteen in June. I had a choice to have a party this year or wait until I was sixteen. Of course, I told them I could wait until I was sixteen. It seemed Britney's parents didn't spare any expense for her party. All of us were in a trance when one of our favorite rappers came out on stage. We chanted along with the crowd, "Soulja Boy."

"Where's the birthday girl?"

"Here I am," Britney screamed. We followed her up on stage. We all danced along as he rapped.

I was having so much fun that I hadn't paid Cameron any attention. After we got off the stage he made a point of coming right up to speak with me. "You got some nice moves there," he said.

"I'm not sure if Lauren told you, but I'm on the dance squad. You'll get to see more of those moves if you come to the football games," I responded.

He opened up his mouth to say something else, but I didn't wait. I moved through the crowd and went to find my girls. They were already sitting at our table. Britney's parents, Jasmine's mom, and a few of Britney's other relatives were in the immediate area. We ate, laughed, and talked. Britney enjoyed being the center of attention. Jasmine and I sat back and watched her as she opened up her gifts. "Sierra, I love them," Britney said, as she unwrapped the Coach handbag and wallet. We hugged. I was glad she was satisfied with my gift. I continued to watch Britney open up the rest of her gifts.

I caught Cameron watching me throughout the night. Since Lauren was his date, I didn't give him any more of my time. I reveled in the attention the other guys at the party were giving me. Even Jasmine seemed surprised that more guys were flirting with me than with her. She would never admit it bothered her, but I could tell from her facial expressions that it did.

Overall, I think Britney's birthday party was a success. She seemed to have a good time. All of us danced until Britney's dad said it was time to shut the party down. People would be talking about Britney's party for weeks to come.

~ 6 ~

Young and Restless

"Back to reality," I sang, as I listened to a song on my iPod while walking to my dance class the Monday following Britney's birthday party.

"Oops," I said, as I accidentally bumped into a girl. "Sorry, I didn't see you."

Marcus Johnson, Britney's ex-boyfriend, and some girl I didn't know turned in my direction. "That's cool," the girl said.

Marcus said, "Sierra, what's up?"

"Trying to get to dance class."

"See you around," Marcus said.

I heard the girl say, "Who was that?"

Marcus responded harshly, "You don't need to

worry about that. Just make sure when I call you, you answer your phone."

I made a mental note to ask Britney if she knew about Marcus' new girlfriend.

After getting dressed for dance class, I drank several glasses of water. I had been feeling dehydrated all day. I knew my dance teacher would be giving us a full workout so I wanted to replenish my fluids.

Britney strolled in late to class. She seemed a little out of it, especially for someone who had a grand birthday celebration. I knew if it had been me, I would still be celebrating. "What's wrong?" I asked as soon as we sat on our mats beside each other.

"Marcus. He's tripping because he didn't get an invite to my party."

"I thought you two were through."

"We are so that's why I can't understand why he's tripping."

"Have you met his new girlfriend?"

"What new girlfriend?"

By now our teacher was looking in our direction. I mouthed the words, "I'll tell you after class."

Britney's reaction made it appear as if she had more feelings for Marcus than she let on. She claimed to not like him like that anymore, but now I had my thoughts. She beat me to the locker room for us to change clothes.

"What's this about a girlfriend?" she asked me, as we changed clothes.

"I assumed it was his new girlfriend," I responded. I told her about the conversation I overheard.

"How does she look?" Britney asked. I don't know what it is about us girls. We always like to compare ourselves with other girls.

"She was a few inches shorter than you. Her hair was cut short like Rihanna's. I guess she's cute. Not as cute as we are, but you know I'm not a dude so who am I to judge?"

Britney seemed to be satisfied with my answer. "Well, good. Now maybe Marcus will stop calling me so much."

I doubt if Britney really meant that. I let the subject drop for the moment. I was quick to do so because on the way to class I got a good view of Cameron and Lauren cuddled up together in front of her locker. When Lauren saw me looking, she looped her arm through Cameron's. Since he didn't bother to move her away, I figured he was okay with it. He looked guilty when he realized I was looking. He bowed his head and pretended that he didn't see me.

"Hi Sierra," Cecil said.

"Do I know you?" I asked. He looked familiar, but I didn't know who he was.

"It's me. Cecil. Remember, I tutored Jasmine in Algebra this past spring," he said.

Oh my goodness. This couldn't be. The Cecil I remembered wore thick glasses. He was nerdy looking. He did not look like the cute guy that stood in front of me. Well, he did resemble Cecil. I looked at Cecil up and down.

He said, "Looks like we both transformed over the summer."

While I was checking him out, Cecil was checking me out. "I lost a few pounds," I admitted.

"You're looking good. Speaking of looking good, how's your friend doing?" he asked.

"Jas is Jas. I'm surprised I'm just now running into you. But then again, you're a junior now aren't you?"

"Yes and I don't care what they tell you. It doesn't get easier. Not only do I have to study for class—I have all these college entrance exams I have to study for."

"You're smart. You'll do alright," I assured him.

"Well tell Jasmine I asked about her. Tell her my number hasn't changed, so she could give me a call sometime."

"I will," I said. We were now near the door of my next class. "Take care."

"You too," he said, as he held the door open for me.

I couldn't wait to message Britney about Cecil. I wondered if Jasmine knew how good he was looking these days. He was smart and cute, so if Jasmine didn't want him, some other girl would, and no, not me. After DJ, we all made a pact to not go after or date any guy who the other person had any remote interest in. Cecil seemed to still have a thing for Jasmine and even in her denial I felt Jasmine was flattered by Cecil's sincere admiration.

After school Britney and I talked about Cecil. Jasmine walked up. "I know you're talking about me because you stopped talking as soon as I got here."

"You have a complex problem," Britney teased.

"Whatever you have to say about me, say it to my face," Jasmine said, as she stood with her hand on her hips.

I said, "Have you seen Cecil lately?"

Jasmine had an irritated look on her face. "No

and why should I care? If I need him for tutoring, I'll call him."

Britney said, "From what Sierra told me, you might want to call him."

"Sierra if you want him, you can have him. You two probably have more in common than I do."

"But . . ." I said.

Jasmine wouldn't allow me to finish. "I'm serious. I don't like Cecil like that. He was my tutor who became a friend. The end." She snapped her fingers to emphasize the point.

Britney said, "You might change your mind when you see him."

"I doubt it. I'm not even worried about Cecil or any other boy for that matter. I'm trying to make sure I don't miss any moves. Those girls are doing their best to get me kicked off the cheerleading team, but I'm not having it."

Britney and I looked from one to the other. This was the first time we had heard about Jasmine having problems with her cheerleading squad. I would have to find out more later because my mom was parked alongside the curb waiting for me when we got outside.

My mom was unusually quiet on the ride home. Before we got to our neighborhood, she finally opened up, but now I wished she hadn't. "Did you tell your dad about our trips?"

"No," I said. It dawned on me why she had been acting funny with me the last few days. She thought I revealed to my dad her little secrets.

"I don't know how he found out but he did. If he asks you anything about us going shopping, do not and I repeat do not let him know anything."

"But he's my dad and I don't feel comfortable lying to him."

My mom said, "Your dad is under enough stress. You telling him about the shopping will only cause more. You love your dad don't you?"

"Of course I do. What kind of question is that?" I was livid.

"If you keep my secret, I'll keep your secret about the Cameron guy you've been doodling about."

~ 7 ~

Back to Being Maria

"There's no secret. Cameron's a guy in one of my classes."

"That's what you tell me. I know about DJ."

My mouth flew open. I had never talked to her about DJ. She went on to say, "Britney's mom told me what happened after you and Jasmine almost ended your friendship over the dude."

"Why didn't you say anything?" I asked.

"Since the problem worked itself out, I didn't have to. Besides, I figured you would come to me if you really needed to."

I wasn't sure where she was going with this conversation. I didn't know what to say. All I could think of was the fact that she knew about DJ all of this time and never said anything. She said, "You know if your dad knew about DJ and now this Cameron guy, he would have a fit. You would be grounded until you graduated."

"But there's no need to tell him about DJ, since he's in the past and like I said, Cameron's just a guy that goes to my school."

"As long as we're on the same page. You keep my little secret and I'll keep yours." She turned the volume up on the stereo. The music blasted but didn't drown out my thoughts.

I stared out the window in disbelief. My own mother, correction, stepmother, just blackmailed me to be silent. I wasn't going to say anything anyway, but Maria had stooped to an all time low. The respect I once had for her was out the window.

When we got home, I headed straight to my room. Zion burst in my door. "How many times do I have to tell you to knock first?" I yelled.

"Mom said dinner will be ready in about an hour."

"Tell your mom I said okay. Now I would appreciate you getting out of my room so I can finish my homework."

"Looks like you were surfing the net to me."

"Get out," I yelled.

"I'm telling mama," Zion responded.

"I don't care. Just get out of my room," I said, as I picked up a pillow on my bed and threw it at him.

Zion ran out of the room slamming the door behind him.

I attempted to get Britney and Jasmine on the phone. Britney was the only one available. "Can you believe she tried to blackmail me?" I asked, after going over the afternoon's events.

Britney said, "You said your father was real upset. She probably didn't mean anything by it. Just try to stay out of their mess."

"It's like I'm in the twilight zone or something. I was cool with everything until she tried to throw DJ in my face."

"Calm down," Britney said.

Being calm was the last thing on my mind. Maria thought my dad was mad at her. She hadn't seen anything yet. I probably shouldn't have snapped at Zion. It's not his fault that his mother was a blackmailer.

Jasmine called me back. "I didn't know your mom had it in her. I like her even more now." Jasmine laughed.

"Well, I don't. And she's not my mom."

Jasmine got serious. "Sierra, she's just looking

out for your dad. He's probably under enough stress. My dad was stressing over losing his dealerships. If he hadn't gotten that commentator job doing Monday Night Football, there's no telling what he would be doing now. We would probably be moving back to Oak Cliff with my mom's sister."

It didn't matter what the situation was, Jasmine always seemed to get the story back on her and whatever was going on in her life. I listened to her go on and on. It temporarily got my mind off my issues. Jasmine could be right. Telling my dad about Maria's excessive shopping would cause more drama. I had already lost one parent. I didn't want to lose another because of stress.

I pretended to be sick when it was time for dinner. Instead, I waited until I knew they were through eating then I made a plate for myself. I made sure I piling the food as high as I could. I hoped to run into Maria so she could see it. That's another thing. I was tired of her sly comments about my weight. I had lost twenty-five pounds but she acted like I hadn't lost any weight. I'm sure if I ate all this food, I would gain some weight. Feeling guilty, I removed most of the food on my plate, leaving only a reasonable amount of food then retreated back to my room.

"You're not supposed to eat in your room," Maria said.

"If you would have knocked first, you wouldn't see me eat," I responded, as I stuffed the fork in my mouth.

"Sierra, I don't know what's gotten into you but you better watch your tone."

"Whatever," I said, under my breath. I rolled my eyes and went back to eating.

"Do I need Jorge to talk to you about your attitude?" she asked.

I stopped eating. I looked Maria dead in the eyes and said, "Do I need to tell dear old dad about your shopping trips?"

Maria's mouth dropped open but no words came out. I said, "I guess we're on the same page then. Maria, please close the door all the way when you leave. I really would like to eat in peace."

Maria sighed loudly and slammed my door when she left. I couldn't do anything but laugh. The look on her face when I pulled one of her numbers was priceless.

~ 8 ~
Two Can Play

"Two can play that game. One difference is I play better than you," I sang the words to one of Parris Mitchell's new songs.

I laughed out loud because I'm sure if Maria listened to the lyrics, she probably thought back to last night.

Maria had been blasting K104 but as soon as I got into that song, she changed it to one of the jazz stations.

"You kids listen to too much junk these days."

"She's about your age. I would think you would be glad I was listening to Parris songs instead of rap."

"Well, she's alright. I just don't like that song. Every time I turn on the radio, they're playing it."

"I love it," I said. Maria changing the station didn't stop me from singing. I put in the earplugs to my iPod and sang as if I was listening to it. I glanced out of the corner of my eye and saw Maria grip the steering wheel harder.

I smiled. *Yes, mama dearest, or should I say Maria. Two can definitely play the game you're trying to play.*

Maria seemed relieved to drop me off at school. I was barely out of the car when she sped away without even telling me her customary good-bye. *Oh, well.* I sat in what my friends and I called "our spot", waiting on Jasmine and Britney to arrive. I pulled out the latest book in the Denim Diaries series.

"That's a nice cover," Cameron said, as he sat next to me.

I closed the book. "It's a good book."

"Maybe I can borrow your copy when you finish."

I held the book close to my heart. "You'll have to get your own copy. This one is autographed. I won't even let my best friends borrow it." I opened up the book so he could see the personalized message on the inside.

"Cool. I'll see if my dad will take me to the book store today."

"If you go to the one on the corner of Preston, I think the author left some autographed copies there."

"But it won't be personalized like your copy."

"At least it'll be autographed," I said.

"Do your parents let you date?" he asked.

"Why?"

"I was wondering if we could go out sometime, maybe this weekend."

I saw Lauren walking in our direction from a distance. I said, "What would Lauren have to say about it?"

"Lauren is not an issue."

"Boo," Jasmine yelled. I jumped. Jasmine and Britney laughed. "Y'all both jumped."

"Cameron these are my two best friends. Although, if they try to scare me again, they will be my two ex-best friends."

Jasmine held out her hand. "Jasmine, but my friends call me Jazzy J."

Britney extended her hand. "And I'm Britney."

Lauren walked by looking our way but she didn't bother to stop. "Hi Cameron," she said, without acknowledging the rest of us.

Cameron seemed to get uncomfortable real quick. A few minutes later, he left and went inside the school doors.

Jasmine said, "I know you might not want to take my advice. But if I were you, I wouldn't give Cameron the time of day. Anybody who would mess around with Lauren is somebody I wouldn't want to fool with."

Britney, always the voice of reason said, "Lauren's not that bad. You just don't like her."

Jasmine responded, "You're absolutely correct. I don't like her, Sierra doesn't like her, and since we're being honest, you don't like her."

Britney couldn't disagree. Lauren was Tanisha's friend. Tanisha and Jasmine got into it several times during our freshman year. She no longer went to our school. She ended up getting pregnant by DJ and the last I heard she and her little boy had moved to Mansfield, Louisiana to live with her grandmother. I don't know what a city girl like Tanisha would do in a small town like Mansfield; but I'm sure milking cows wouldn't be one of them.

We headed to homeroom. I purposely walked by

Cameron when I entered the classroom. Lauren frowned and turned around folding her arms.

My phone vibrated. I sneaked and took a look before Ms. Hogan came in the room. It was Jasmine sending me a text message. It read, "Was all that necessary." She ended the text with "LOL—laughing out loud."

Lauren couldn't keep her eyes off me. She was rolling them so much, I was afraid they would fall on the floor. I flashed a smile and made a point of moving my head so that my long hair would fall over my shoulders. If looks could kill, Lauren would have placed a dagger upside of my head.

Ms. Hogan rushed in the room. "Sorry, I'm late. You all can put your books away. Take one and pass it down," she said, as she handed the head of each row some stapled papers.

I was not prepared for a pop quiz in geography. I scanned the papers before attempting to answer any of the questions. Fortunately, I knew the answers to all of the questions. I received a perfect score on the quiz. Jasmine and Britney both missed one. They weren't upset because they still got an A.

"How did you do?" I asked Lauren in front of Cameron. I knew she had a D because I graded her paper.

She mumbled something. I said, "What? I didn't hear you."

"A D. I didn't have time to study."

Cameron said, "I got a B. I got stumped on that last question."

I faced Cameron. "Well if you ever need help, let me know. I tutor."

Lauren said, "What about me? I'm the one with the D, not him."

I ignored her and left them to go to my next class. While on the way to class I saw Cecil. Of course the first thing out of his mouth was questions about Jasmine. I said, "I told her what you said, but Cecil between you and me, she's a lost cause. Count your losses and move on."

"I really like her. She's everything I want in a girl," he said. My heart dropped when I saw the pain in Cecil's eyes. I don't know what came over me. I hugged him.

Cecil gained his composure and pulled away. He sniffled a little. "I'll be alright. Thanks for the advice." He walked away looking like a lost puppy.

"Who was that?" Britney asked, as we bumped into each other.

"Mister Cecil."

"Talk about a transformation. He got rid of the glasses. He's looking hot."

"Told you," I said.

"Who's looking hot?" Jasmine asked, as she walked in on the tail end of our conversation.

Britney said, "Somebody you said you were no longer interested in."

"Who? Come on now," Jasmine said.

"Cecil."

Jasmine burst out laughing. "I'm not even falling for it. Cecil is cute in a nerdy sort of way, but hot, no way, no how."

Britney said, "Okay, but don't say we didn't warn you."

~ 9 ~

Practice Makes Perfect

"One . . . two . . . one . . . two . . . three . . . step," Ms. Vernon, our new dance squad leader chanted. "Now with the music."

Britney and I learned our new dance routines for the Dancing Diamonds in a short period of time. We were now in our fourth week of school. Homecoming was right around the corner. Ms. Vernon insisted on us rehearsing every day after school since we were scheduled to perform at not only the pep rally for homecoming but during the halftime festivities. I couldn't wait. Now that I had lost some weight, I was prancing around the dance floor even more. Some of the upperclassman on the squad didn't like the fact that Ms. Vernon appointed me co-captain.

"If that heifer rolls her eyes at me one more time, I swear I'm going to go upside her head," I said.

"You're sounding so much like Jasmine these days," Britney said.

"I'm just saying. I don't mess with nobody. I come to rehearsal. I learn my routine and I leave. Why are they acting like that?"

Britney wouldn't look me in the eyes when she talked. "Maybe it's the way you've been acting like you're the only one who knows the moves."

I threw my hands up in the air. "Not you too, Bri. I just want to make sure we're on point. Ms. Vernon has placed me as co-captain so I'm going to make sure our squad is good."

Britney said, "We are good."

"Well you know what I mean."

Britney said, "All I'm saying is, you should tone things down. Stop acting like you're the only one out there who can dance. Concentrate on what the other girls are doing right and maybe, just maybe, things will go a little bit more smoothly."

I heard Britney but didn't listen because it was

not my role to pacify their egos. My job was to make sure they did the dance routines to the best of their abilities and that's exactly what I was going to do. I was not there to make friends. Besides, I think they were now jealous because I was no longer the fattest chick on the squad.

During lunch the next day, Jasmine finally saw Cecil. Cecil stopped by the table to speak. Surprisingly, he ignored Jasmine and spoke directly to me. After Cecil had left our table, Jasmine said, "Oh my goodness, he must have taken some growth pills. His body is . . ."

"More defined," Britney added.

"He's no longer wearing those glasses. He took my advice." Jasmine seemed astonished.

"You're singing a new tune now aren't you?" I teased her.

Jasmine pretended Cecil hadn't captured her attention, but Britney and I knew she was faking.

Later that day, Jasmine went to cheerleading practice, while Britney and I went to dance practice. The members of my dance squad might not like me as much as they did last year, but each had to admit that we were living up to the name of Dancing Diamonds because our routine was flawless. Two hours later, my dance coach said, "Good job. That's it for today ladies."

"Who are you going to the homecoming dance with?" one of the girls on the squad asked as I walked to the locker room to change back into our clothes.

"I haven't decided," I lied. Up until this point, I hadn't thought about it.

Britney was changing back into her school uniform when I saw her. I asked, "Who are you going to the homecoming dance with?"

"I'm not sure."

"So you've been asked?" I was feeling left out. I thought we were girls. Why hadn't she told me she had been asked out? Those questions and more ran through my head.

"I hadn't said anything because it's no big deal." Britney looped one of her arms through her backpack strap.

I was almost through changing clothes. "Well, I haven't been asked."

"Give it some time," she said. "Hey, let me go see if Brenda's out there so she won't try to leave us."

I wondered if Jasmine had a date. Britney said give it more time, but the homecoming dance was less than two weeks away. Guys had been check-ing me out, but no one had asked me to the dance. I looked at my reflection in the full length mirror. My thighs were thick and the flab on my behind didn't seem like it was going anywhere. I really liked Cameron but he was hanging around Lauren. Looking at my body and comparing it to Lauren's I knew I didn't stand a chance if that's the kind of girl he wanted to go out with. I probably looked like an Amazon compared to her. The twenty-five pounds I lost over the summer wasn't enough. I was determined to lose more weight.

My cell phone rang. It was Jasmine. "I'm com-ing," I said, as soon as I answered the phone.

As I got in the back of Brenda's mustang, Brenda said "I've been meaning to tell you. I like your hair straight."

"Thanks," I responded.

For some reason Britney didn't talk much as Brenda drove us home. When we first got in the car, Jasmine talked non-stop about cheerleading practice. I barely listened to her. I was too con-cerned about Britney's attitude. I don't know what Britney's problem was but I wasn't in the mood to deal with her, especially since I had to deal with

Maria once I got home. Jasmine and Britney chatted while I looked out the window.

When I got dropped off, Britney acted like she could barely open up her mouth to say bye. I blew it off as I drudgingly entered the house. To my relief, I made it to my room without running into Maria. Less than thirty minutes later, someone knocked on my door.

"Come in," I yelled.

"You don't know how to tell someone you're home?" Maria asked, as she stood in the doorway with one hand on her hip.

"I figured you were busy," I lied.

Maria looked around right before walking in my room. She moved my notebooks out of the way and took a seat on the bed. I kept my head buried in my English book, the entire time thinking, *Will she leave me alone?*

"Since you've resorted to calling me Maria, I know you're upset with me."

I looked up briefly and then back down at my book. Maria continued to say, "I should have done this before but I'm woman enough to admit my mistakes."

She got my attention. I stopped pretending like I was reading and continued to remain quiet.

Maria said, "I want to apologize for throwing up DJ in your face. Things have been strained with your dad. I felt like my back was against the wall."

"Okay," was all I managed to say. She was not getting off that easy.

She reached over and placed her hand over mine. "Do you forgive me?"

"Maria, it really hurt me when you did that. It made me look at you a whole lot differently." Since we were being honest, I felt she needed to know.

She pulled me into a hug. I let her, but didn't hug her back. "Give it some time and we'll be right back on track. Your dad will be here shortly so I'm going to go finish cooking. I hope you eat dinner with us tonight."

I shrugged my shoulders. Maria said, "Pleee-asse."

"I'll be there."

Maria stood up probably feeling assured that things were well between us, but things really weren't. "I'll send Zion up here when it's ready."

She left me alone with my thoughts. At times like this I wished my mom were still alive. My dad said I looked just like her. I didn't think so because from the pictures I had seen, my mom, whose name was Vanessa, was beautiful. My dad also mentioned she was a great dancer. I guess that's where I got my moves from because my dad had no rhythm.

If I wasn't still mad at Maria, I would say as a stepmom she's alright, a little overbearing, but alright. I would probably forgive her eventually, but for now, I would let her squirm.

~ 10 ~
A Thin Line

"Sierra, wait up. Let me talk to you for a minute," Cameron said, after homeroom the next morning. "Bri and Jas, I'll see y'all at lunch."

Britney and Jasmine walked away but not without looking back at me and Cameron.

"What's up?" I asked.

"Are you going to the homecoming dance?" he asked.

Of course I wanted to go and I wanted to go with Cameron. My heart skipped a beat because one of my dreams was coming true. Cameron was asking me to the dance.

"I plan on going," I responded. I think I held my breath as I waited for him to ask me.

"Cool. Well make sure you save me a dance," Cameron said.

"Excuse me," I said out loud before I could catch myself. *Did he just not ask me to the homecoming dance?*

"Save me a dance. Ooops, I'm running late for class. I can't afford another tardy," he said.

Just like that, Cameron had built me up and burst my bubble when he didn't ask me to go to the dance with him. I felt like eating a double burger loaded with everything and a whole bunch of fries but I knew that wouldn't accomplish anything. It would only make me have to work extra hard on losing the weight I would have gained by eating it.

The rest of my morning dragged on as I thought about my disappointing encounter with Cameron. I saw him and Lauren walking into the cafeteria. Although I had been getting the attention of a lot of the boys lately, there was no way I could compete with Lauren's size. I would never be a size three. So I guess that means I would never get Cameron. The thought of it depressed me. "What's up chica?" Britney said, as she walked up behind me in the serving line.

"Nothing," I said.

"Cheer up because I have some great news. I finally decided on who I'm going to the homecoming dance with."

I pretended to care. "Who?"

"Luther Smalls."

"The guy on the football team?" I asked.

"The one and same. Can you believe it? He could go out with any girl, but he chose me," Britney said. She went on and on about it until we made it to our designated table.

I pretended to be excited too. On the inside, I felt more depressed. There was no way I could tell her about my encounter with Cameron now. When Jasmine arrived, Britney repeated her story to her.

"He is such a cutie. I'm jealous," Jasmine said, as she opened up her straw to put in her juice.

"Have you decided who you are going with?" Britney asked.

"I decided to go with Luther's team mate, Reggie."

Jasmine and Britney went on and on about how fine they thought Reggie and Luther were. I picked at my food. Throwing in an occasional fake smile when I thought they were looking in my direction.

"What should I wear?" Jasmine asked.

"I'm wearing something red, because you know I look good in red," Britney said.

Jasmine asked, "What about you Sierra?"

What? They were now trying to include me in on the conversation. I couldn't believe it. When I looked up from my plate, both pair of eyes were on me. "I haven't decided on whether or not I am going yet."

Jasmine said, "You have to go. It won't be any fun without all three of us there."

Britney said, "She's right. You have to. If you need me to get your dress, I can do that."

"Things aren't that bad at home where I can't get my own dress," I said.

"I'm just saying. Why don't you want to go?" Britney asked.

"If you guys haven't noticed I don't have a date."

Jasmine said, "Well why didn't you say so? We can hook you up with somebody."

I rolled my eyes. "I don't think so. I don't need a hook up. I can get a date on my own thank you." I said it like I meant it, but I really wasn't so sure. If I could get a date on my own, then I wouldn't be the only one of my friends without a date to the homecoming dance.

Britney said, "Between the two of us, we'll find you someone."

There's a thin line between being a friend and being a nuisance. Right now Britney and Jasmine had definitely crossed the line into being a nuisance. "No, okay. If I get a date, I'll come. If not, I'll chill at the house and wait for you two to tell me all about it later."

I threw my items on the tray and left the table without waiting on Britney and Jasmine. I rushed out of the cafeteria almost knocking Cecil down. "Slow down or you're going to hurt somebody," he yelled, as I brushed past him.

I retreated to the rest room. I fumbled through my backpack in search of a tube of lip gloss. I pulled out the tube Jasmine had given me earlier. I threw it back in the backpack. "This is the one I want," I said out loud.

Britney and Jasmine entered the bathroom as I puckered up my lips and ran the brush across them with cherry lip gloss.

Britney approached me and said, "We're sorry. If you don't want our help, we'll stay out of it."

I looked at their reflections in the mirror. "I don't need a pity date."

Jasmine said, "It wouldn't be a pity date. Girl

you're looking real good these days. Finding you a date isn't going to be a problem, so stop thinking of it like that."

I said, "The answer is still no. If I get a date, fine. If not, it wasn't meant for me to go to the dance."

~ 11 ~

Homecoming

Britney and Jasmine spent the majority of the week pleading with me to let them find me a date. They had no idea how it made me feel to know that even with all the weight I had lost no one had asked me out. *I might as well be fatter. At least then I would know it was because of my weight.*

I blocked out the homecoming dance and concentrated on my dance routine for the homecoming game. I made it up in my mind that I would be so good during my one minute solo performance that the guys who didn't ask me, would have wished they had, especially Cameron.

It was the day before the big game, so we were

set to perform at the pep rally. The pep rally was going on strong when the Dancing Diamonds were called out to hype up the crowd. We had the whole crowd on their feet by the end of our performance. I walked right past Lauren when I exited the floor. She leaned over and said something to one of her friends. They both pointed at me and started laughing. I don't know what was said, but it didn't phase me. I might not be confident in a lot of areas, but my dancing ability was not one of them. I knew we, especially me, had gotten down out there on the gymnasium floor.

I listened as Ms. Vernon gave us instructions for tomorrow's game. She said, "I want you here an hour before the game. If you're late, you won't be performing. Understood?"

We all responded, "Yes, ma'am."

Britney and I went back to the stands. We watched Jasmine from a distance and cheered from the stands showing our support for Jasmine and the rest of the cheerleaders who were prancing around on the gymnasium floor. Jasmine saw us as she was leaving the floor and waved. She used her hand to indicate she wanted one of us to call her.

Guys were checking us out, but since none of those guys had taken the time to ask me to the homecoming dance, I ignored them. Britney stopped and flirted with a few. I kept on walking. She caught up with me just as we got near Lauren and her clique. I overheard Lauren say, "Cameron is picking me up in a limousine tomorrow night." I knew she was saying it for my benefit, but I didn't care. I kept on walking as if I didn't hear her. Her friends sounded impressed. I wasn't.

Britney sent Jasmine a quick text message to let her know we would be waiting outside the gym. Cecil came out of the gym and spoke to me before going to his next class. Britney said, "I think he likes you."

"Don't say that in front of Jasmine," I said.

"Don't say what?" Jasmine asked, as she walked up to us from behind.

Britney beat me to saying, "Nothing. Come on let's go before we're late for our next class."

We talked about how hyped the crowd had been during both of our performances before we all separated to go to our last class of the day. I thought about what Britney said about Cecil. I doubt if he liked me. He just preferred talking to me over Britney about Jasmine. Like I told Cecil before, he was wasting his time. He should find some other girl to fascinate himself with. I should take my own advice. It sure seemed like my attraction to Cameron was a moot point since he and Lauren seem to be a couple.

I was still thinking about Cameron when I entered math class. I did my best to concentrate on the lecture but failed. My math teacher paused when one of the ladies from the office entered. She whispered something in his ear. Mr. Daniels said, "Sierra, go with Ms. Roberts please."

I hoped nothing happened to my dad. "Bring your stuff," Ms. Roberts said.

I did as instructed, packing up my book and notebooks then placing them in my backpack.

"Ms. Hogan needs to see you right away," Ms. Roberts said, once we were out of the room.

"What did I do? I've been showing up on time. I don't think I've been tardy once," I exclaimed.

"Believe me; you'll be happy about this."

Ms. Roberts didn't say anything else to me as we headed to Ms. Hogan's office. When we arrived there, Ms. Roberts and the sophomore Student Body president Michelle Sparks were in deep conversation. I waited for them to finish before entering the room.

Ms. Hogan stood up. "Have a seat. We have some great news for you."

I threw my backpack on the floor beside the chair I would be sitting on. I looked back and forth between her and Michelle.

Michelle spoke first. "It looks like your peers want you to represent them as the sophomore homecoming queen. The votes are in and you were on the ballot."

I sat in shock then I blurted out, "I thought Stacy was chosen as the homecoming queen."

"She was but according to our bylaws, she can't be selected because of her age. This is her second year being a sophomore. You were the runner-up."

"Wow," was all I could say. "I can't believe this."

Ms. Hogan said, "If you can't afford a dress, I have a hook up at Macy's."

Some people had no clue that my dad, although a penny pincher, had money. I didn't need any charity; at least I hoped I didn't. "My dad will take care of it. I just don't have time. Today's the dance. Tomorrow's the game. Is there someone else you can pick?"

Ms. Hogan said, "You're going to be just fine."

My hand flew up to my head. "My hair. What am I going to do with my hair?"

Michelle said, "You have some beautiful hair. Pin it up or flat iron it."

They were taking away all of the excuses I could come up with. I couldn't wait to tell Britney and Jasmine about this. I was floating on a cloud. Even the sight of Cameron and Lauren together in the hallway didn't faze me. Britney and Jasmine were waiting for me outside.

"Looks like I'll be going to the dance after all. I'm sophomore queen," I blurted out.

Instead of being excited for me, Jasmine asked, "How did that happen?"

Britney made up for Jasmine's lack of excitement, by hugging me and we jumped up and down. Jasmine's facial expression said it all. Jealousy didn't look cute on her at all.

~ 12 ~
The Royal Court

Maria was all too happy to have an excuse to take me shopping. My dad seemed happy about me being queen but I could tell he was apprehensive when he gave Maria strict instructions on keeping within a certain budget.

"Dear, I'll do my best. She's a queen so she has to look the part," Maria said, as she and I left to go to her favorite specialty dress shop.

During the ride over to the store, Maria said, "See, I told you life would be different for you if you lose weight."

Life was different alright. I might have been voted queen but I was a queen without her king. I still had no official date to the homecoming dance.

I found a dress that was within the price range my dad had given us. Maria and I walked out with a beautiful off-white dress adorned with beads and crystals that sparkled like diamonds. Maria insisted on getting herself a few items, but that was no concern of mine. That was between her and my dad. It seemed with everything being last minute, I had to rush to get ready. With Maria's help, I liked what stared back at me in the mirror. My hair and dress looked flawless.

My dad was waiting in the living room with his camera. "You behave yourself," my dad said, as he stood teary-eyed, in between taking pictures.

"Yes sir."

The doorbell rang. I wondered who it could be. I told Jasmine and Britney I would meet them at the dance. A man dressed up in a black uniform appeared. My dad said, "I thought my princess, correction, the sophomore queen, deserved to go to the dance in style."

"Daddy, thank you," I said, as I hugged him.

Maria tried to pull me away from my dad. "Don't mess up your hair dear. Now remember what I said. Smile. Even if your shoes start hurting, smile."

I attempted to calm my nerves. "I'll be home by midnight I promise."

"You'll turn into a pumpkin if you don't," Zion said and laughed.

"Whatever, knucklehead. Don't go in my room," I instructed him.

I followed the driver to the black stretch limousine. I felt like Cinderella as he opened the door and I stepped into the empty limousine. I tried to focus on the positive side as he drove me to the Renaissance Hotel in Richardson, a few miles from our school, and where our homecoming dance was being held.

All eyes were on me when the limousine pulled up. "Here's my card just in case you want to leave before midnight. I won't be far," the driver assured me.

I took the card and placed it in the cute little handbag Maria let me borrow. Some of my schoolmates stared as I entered the hotel. Cameron and Lauren were the first two people I recognized upon entering the hotel lobby. "Hi. You look lovely," Cameron said. Lauren rolled her eyes.

"Thanks." I didn't wait around to see if he had anything else to say. I made a point of looking Lauren up and down before stepping away. I used my hand and flung my ringlets over my shoulder.

I laughed to myself when I heard Lauren tell Cameron, "Are you with her or me?"

Britney and Jasmine were both dressed fabulously as usual. Britney flaunted around in her cute red strapless dress. Jasmine still didn't seem to warm up to the idea that I was going to be crowned queen tonight. "For a rush job, you look nice," she seemed to force herself to say.

"Thanks. I think," I responded.

Jasmine looped her arm through her dates arm. "Well, we want to take pictures before the line gets too long. You're welcome to come too."

"I'll pass. I'm sure there will be enough pictures taken for me to remember this occasion once I'm crowned Queen." I turned and walked away not waiting to hear what her or Britney had to say.

The deejay played some of the latest songs and kept the dance floor packed. I sat and observed everybody having a good time. *I'm supposed to be queen but at this time I don't feel like it.* The deejay turned the music down and announced the crowning of the homecoming court. I looked around to see if Britney or Jasmine was around. My eyes found them standing in the picture line. I held my head down as I made my way closer to the stage.

My friends should have been happy for me. Instead it seemed they were too engrossed with their dates to care.

We lined up according to class. I did as Maria suggested and plastered a smile on my face. I was smiling on the outside, but felt like crying on the inside. I did start feeling better when my name was announced. I carefully walked across the stage and was officially crowned Sophomore Homecoming Queen. I was handed a bouquet of red roses. Camera lights flashed from several directions. I made the customary walk across the stage and waved to the audience. I couldn't see the audience faces with the light beaming on the stage. I stood next to the guy who had been crowned Sophomore Homecoming King.

A girl who must have been his date bombarded him as soon as we exited the stage. Everyone had someone waiting for them once they left the stage, except for me. I continued to smile as if all was well in my world. Now that the crowning ceremony was over, I was ready to go. My two best friends had abandoned me. I felt so all alone. I quickly learned that being thinner didn't necessarily mean life would be better.

"Smile," Cecil said. He held up his camera as I walked past him.

I stopped and posed. Cecil acted as if he was a professional photographer and I was his model. "I'm about to get out of here," I said.

"Where's your girl?" he asked.

I pointed back towards the entranceway to the dance area. "She's in there somewhere."

"Is she by herself?" he asked.

I leaned back and crossed my arms. "Now you know better than to ask me that."

"Just being hopeful."

I chatted with Cecil for a few more minutes before leaving the homecoming dance. Britney had called my cell phone several times. When I didn't answer her calls, Jasmine called. I ignored them both. *Now they want to be concerned about me.*

~ 13 ~

Game Over

My dad and Maria had an event hosted by the Dallas mayor to go to so they would not be at the homecoming game. I was a little disappointed they couldn't be at my first performance, but my dad had explained how he needed to be there to network, especially since the real estate business had been slow lately.

Britney and Jasmine's families showed up. I felt alone since none of my family was there. Even though I was still mad at Maria, I would have been fine with her and my little brother there to cheer me on. *Oh well, I'll have to show them the video.* According to Britney, her dad would be filming us.

I was still a little disappointed with Britney and Jasmine, but I pretended all was well between us.

We could hear the excitement in the crowd as we waited for instructions on entering the stadium. The announcer introduced us right after the band made its way to the field. I led one of our dance routines. The captain of our squad led the rest of the dance numbers. We exited the field and the band did their thing. After the Dancing Diamonds stellar performance, I changed into another dress since I had to go sit with the other people in the homecoming court. In a way I was glad because I really didn't feel like talking with Britney. Jasmine, as a cheerleader, remained down near the field.

"One of my boys wanted me to introduce you," the sophomore king said, as we watched the game.

"Tell me about him," I said, just to pass the time.

"He's not as good looking as I am, but girls seem to like him."

"How old is he?"

"He's seventeen. He goes to Mesquite High. He's somewhere out in the stands."

I knew there was no way in the world my dad would let me go out with a seventeen year old.

"He's too old for me. Now if he was maybe sixteen, but seventeen, no way," I said.

"He looks younger so your parents wouldn't even trip," he responded.

"You don't know my dad. Knowing him, he would do a background check."

"Oh. I'll text him and let him know."

I watched him send his friend a text message.

He looked up at me and said, "He said it's all good. He understands. He just wanted you to know you make J-Lo look like a booger wolf."

"A what?"

He repeated himself. I burst out laughing. "Your friend is crazy," I said in between laughing.

The score of the game was tied. From where I was sitting, it appeared as if our team's coach was sweating. He called a last minute time out. The noise level from the crowd decreased as we all anticipated the next play. I cheered as our team made the winning touchdown with only seconds left on the clock. The other team knew the game was over. Our boys went out on the field and so did some of the fans from the stands. I was supposed to be riding with Britney so I found my way to where Britney's Dad, mega music producer Teddy Franklin, was parked.

"You looked so cute out there," Destiny Franklin, Britney's mom said.

"Thanks Ms. Destiny," I responded.

"You girls are growing up so fast. I don't know what I'm going to do with y'all," Teddy said.

I blushed. Britney didn't like for us to talk about her dad, but on a hot meter, Mr. Teddy was off the meter. He used to be the lead singer in this successful R & B group. Now he made his money by acquiring artists for a record company. Many artists would give their right arm to be a part of his roster.

"Ms. Pearl has cooked up a feast for you girls," Destiny said, as Jasmine, Britney and I chatted in the back seat of their SUV. Ms. Pearl was the Franklin's cook. The recession didn't seem to be affecting the Franklin household.

Jasmine said, "I'm starving because I was too nervous to eat before the game."

"Me too," I added.

"I hope she baked some cookies. I can taste the mouth-watering chocolate chips now," Britney said.

"I'm sure she'll be glad you ladies will be coming with a healthy appetite," Destiny said.

"That's my jam," Britney said, as her dad blasted a new song.

Jasmine and I had never heard it. "Who is it?" Jasmine asked.

Teddy responded, "That's Mario's new cut. You should be hearing it in heavy rotation soon."

Mario's new song sounded good. I couldn't wait to hear the rest of his CD. By the time we reached Britney's place, I had forgotten that I was supposed to be mad at her and Jasmine for their lack of support.

~ 14 ~

Plano's Most Wanted

The Monday after the game, I seemed to be on everybody's most wanted list. Not only did a few guys slip me their phone numbers, some of the girls were striking up conversation trying to be my friend. I took a seat across from Jasmine and Britney during lunch period.

Jasmine commented, "You seem to be Ms. Popular today."

I shrugged it off. "People are just congratulating me for being queen."

Britney said, "You were cute standing up there."

"Oh you saw me. I thought you two were too busy with your dates to even notice."

"We tried to get your attention, but I guess the light was too bright for you to see us," Jasmine said.

"We called you later too because Cecil told us you had left," Britney said.

"I only went to the dance because of the crowning."

Britney and Jasmine looked at each other. Jasmine folded her arms and leaned back in her chair. Britney leaned forward. "If you would have let us fix you up with someone, you wouldn't have had to go to the dance by yourself."

I threw my hands up in the air. "You just don't get it do you. I don't want to be fixed up. I want the guy to want me for me. Not because one of my friends laid a guilt trip on him so he would go out with poor ol' Sierra."

Jasmine cleared her throat. "As much as I hate to admit this Sierra, it wouldn't be a pity date. I guess you don't notice how the guys seem to be paying you a lot of attention these days. The reason why you didn't get asked is because they probably feel you're unapproachable."

Britney said, "She has a point. Since you've lost weight, you seem to have your head stuck in the sky."

"Excuse me?"

"I didn't stutter," Britney said.

Jasmine commented, "When I see you these days, it's like looking at my own reflection."

"Now you're insulting me," I responded. I was not going to sit there and take their verbal abuse.

"You should be flattered," Jasmine said. "But you know there could only be one me. So as your friends, we want you to know you need to check yourself."

"I can't believe what I'm hearing," I responded.

Britney said, "Sierra, we love you, so don't trip."

"I got to go." I picked up my backpack and left the table before I said something that would have probably ended our friendship. *How dare they talk to me like that?*

"Sierra, can we talk for a moment?" Cecil stopped and asked before I walked out of the cafeteria.

I looked behind me and saw Jasmine and Britney looking in my direction. I responded, "Sure. You can talk as you walk me to class."

"I have a plan on how to get Jasmine to like me but I need your help."

I threw my hand up in protest. "Whatever it is, I do not want to get involved."

Cecil looked at me with his big cute brown eyes and said, "Please. I can't do it without you."

Against my better judgment, I asked, "What's your plan?"

Cecil said, "If she starts seeing me with another

girl that will make her jealous. Then she'll want to talk to me."

"I'm not too sure about that. Jasmine's been pretty adamant about not wanting to talk to you like that."

"But . . ." Cecil stuttered.

"I told you dude, you need to cut your losses and move on. Find you another girl who can care for you the same way you care about her. Jasmine is not the one."

"Someone like you," he said.

"Uh. No. I wasn't talking about me," I stuttered.

Cecil's eyes sparkled when he said, "What if Jasmine thought you and I were dating? Do you think she would call me then?"

I opened up the classroom door. "Believe me, that's not a good idea. If you want her, dating me would not be wise."

"We wouldn't really be dating. We would be pretending. Come on. Think about it."

I left Cecil outside of the classroom pondering his situation. There was nothing to think about in my opinion. Jasmine said she didn't like Cecil like that, but I think she did. Although Jasmine had made me mad, I would not go out with a guy she was remotely interested in. Our friendship almost ended last year because we both went after DJ. I did not want a repeat incident on my hands.

After class, Cameron ran up next to me. "Just the girl I wanted to see."

I was Plano's most wanted today. "What's up?"

"I heard you were good in math. I have a Calculus test coming up and I need some help."

"Sure, I can help you with that. What's your number?" I asked.

He wrote it down on a piece of paper and handed it to me. "I really appreciate this Sierra."

"No problem. I'll have my friend Cecil give you a call so y'all can work out a schedule."

"Cecil?" he asked.

"Yes. Cecil. He's real good at tutoring and math is his specialty. I'm sure if he has the time, he wouldn't mind helping."

"But . . ." Cameron stammered.

"Oops. Look at the time. Besides, there goes your girlfriend."

I heard him say, "She's not my girlfriend," as I continued to walk away. As much as he and Lauren hung together, she might as well have been his girlfriend in my opinion.

~ 15 ~

The Set Up

I saw Cecil right before leaving the building for the day. I placed a piece of paper in his hand. "He needs help with calculus."

Cecil looked at the number. "Who is this?"

"Just some dude I like who hangs out with someone I don't like."

"I'll tutor him, if you'll do me the favor I asked you earlier."

What's up with folks trying to blackmail me? First Maria, now Cecil. I held my "talk to the hand" pose up in the air. "I'm doing great in my calculus class. Whether you help him or not, is between the two of y'all."

I walked away. Cecil ran to catch up to me. "Sierra, I'm sorry. I didn't mean anything by it."

"No biggie. Just call him if you can. If you can't, trash the number."

The sunshine beamed bright in my face as I walked out the school doors. I reached into my backpack and took out my shades. I looked around and saw Britney and Jasmine waiting for me near the sidewalk. Maria was parked on the opposite end. Britney waved to get my attention. I started to pretend I didn't see them. Instead of stooping to their immature level, I acknowledged them and walked over to see what they wanted.

"We're sorry about earlier," Britney said.

"Yeah, do you forgive us?" Jasmine asked, as she pouted out her lips.

"I'll think about it," I said. I wasn't going to let them off the hook too easily.

"We just want our old friend back," Jasmine said.

"I'm the same person. Why do people keep saying I've changed?" I asked.

"Because you have," Britney said. "But we like you anyway." She hugged me.

"Wow. Thanks. I think," I responded, as I hugged her and Jasmine.

I felt my cell phone vibrate inside my backpack. I took it out and looked at the caller ID to see who was rescuing me from my uncomfortable conversation. "That's Maria. Let me go before she has a fit."

"Call us later," Jasmine said.

I threw up my two fingers in the peace sign and walked right in front of Cecil and Cameron talking. I ignored them both and headed to Maria's car.

By the time I got to the car, Maria asked, "What took you so long?"

"We had something to discuss," I said, as I threw my backpack on the back seat.

"I have food cooking so we need to hurry back before the house burns down," Maria said.

After dinner, I returned to my room to finish studying just in case I had any surprise quizzes. I had dozed off to sleep when my phone rang. "What's up?" an unfamiliar voice asked me from the other end.

I asked, "Who is this?"

"Guess," The unknown caller said.

"Either you tell me who you are or I'm hanging up this phone." I positioned myself on my pillows in the bed.

"It's me. Cecil."

"You sound different on the phone," I said. *Wait*

a minute. How did he get my number? I never gave it to him.

"I would recognize your voice anywhere," Cecil said.

I asked, "How did you get my number?"

"Jasmine gave it to me."

"Really?" I said. I was surprised. "How did you convince her to do that?"

"Easy. I told her if she gave it to me, I would stop calling her."

Interesting. "She believed you?"

"Yep. And guess what else?"

"I don't know if I want to know," I responded.

"I told her there was another girl I was interested in and she was happy for me." It sounded like Cecil was smiling through the phone.

"Did you tell her who the girl was?"

"Of course. That's how I was able to get your number."

"What did you tell her?" I asked, holding my breath. "I told her that since she didn't want to talk to me, that maybe you would. That you seem nice enough. See, all of this is a part of my plan."

I cut Cecil off. "I'm not going to be a part of it. I told you that earlier."

"Jasmine thought we would be good for each other. She said you were having a hard time finding a boyfriend and since I was looking for a girlfriend, that maybe we could help each other out."

I was livid. "She said what?"

"Jas was probably upset that I asked her for your number. See the plan is working already."

"Yeah right," I responded. I wondered why Jasmine would say something so hateful. I could find my own boy to talk to. I did not need her pity. The nerve of her trying to set me up with her reject; not that there was anything wrong with Cecil; it was just the principles behind the matter.

Cecil interrupted my thoughts. "Hear me out. I talked to your boy Cameron. He's only fooling around with Lauren because she's giving up the goodies. People can tell you're a good girl so he knows he can't come to you like that."

"How did you find that out?" I asked out of curiosity.

"Guys talk."

Cecil wasn't as nerdy as Jasmine made him out to be. I listened to him as he told me more about what he thought of Cameron. I asked, "Do you think I stand a real chance with him?"

"He likes you, but like I said, he knows he can't

go there with you; so he's doing like a lot of boys, going for the easy prey."

"I thought he didn't want to talk to me because of my weight."

Cecil said, "Sierra, how do I say this without offending you?"

"Just say it," I responded.

"I don't know a boy at Plano High who doesn't think you're fionne- with a capital F."

"Really?"

"Stop acting all surprised. You should know by now you got it going on," he responded.

I laughed out loud. "Cecil you're the first guy who's told me that."

"Well it's true. You had it going on even before you lost all the weight."

"Thank you for the compliment but I still won't do it."

"Is there anything I can do to change your mind?" Cecil asked.

"Nope."

"Okay, just checking. Well, do you mind if I call you sometime? You know, when I'm sitting at home bored and alone and don't want to play any video games because I need some human interaction."

"You sure talk a lot," I said.

"That's what everyone tells me. I can't help it. I just have a lot to say."

"Sure. Call me whenever you feel like it," I said.

As soon as our phone conversation ended, I hit the speed dial for Jasmine. She had some explaining to do and it couldn't wait.

~ 16 ~
Emerald Green

"So how did it go?" Jasmine asked me before even saying hello.

Since she wanted to get straight to the point, I returned the favor and said, "You should have asked me before giving my number out."

"I figured you wouldn't mind. Cecil's good people you know."

"He's interested in you."

"Girl, not any more. I was relieved to learn he wasn't. He can be your problem." I could hear Jasmine blowing a bubble on the other end.

"Can you please stop smacking that gum? It's so irritating," I said.

"What is your problem? You should be glad I

sent Cecil your way. Now you don't have to worry about who you're going to the Sadie's Hawkins Dance with."

"News flash. I don't need your help finding a guy to go out with. I can find one on my own, thank you very much."

"I don't know if I like the new and supposedly improved Sierra."

"Well frankly Jas, I don't care."

"Call me back when you calm down," Jasmine said, before hanging up the phone.

I dialed Britney's number. She didn't answer at first but called me right back. I told her about what happened. She remained so quiet, I had to ask, "Are you there?"

"Yes. I'm here but I don't know what to say to you. Do you like Cecil?"

'No. I like Cameron." *If they paid attention to me, she would know. Sometimes I felt like the invisible friend.*

"Then I don't see what the big deal is."

"Jasmine and probably you think that I can't get a guy on my own. How do you think that's supposed to make me feel?"

Britney said, "You know Jas is Jas. She always

has to make someone else look worse in order to feel better. She's probably tripping that Cecil called her for your number."

I thought about it. If Jasmine did like Cecil, I could see her responding the way she did. *Maybe I did overreact.*

"Between you and me, Cecil is only doing it to make Jasmine jealous. He has no interest in me whatsoever."

"Then you have nothing to worry about. In fact, if Jasmine gave him your number, even if he did like you, Jas would be cool with it. I'm sure."

"Yeah right. I can see emerald green in her eyes sometimes. Jasmine's jealousy is no joke."

"Hold on a minute."

I started removing my fingernail polish while I waited on Britney to come back to the phone. She took so long to come back that if it hadn't been for my head crooked over holding the phone, I would have forgotten she was on the line.

"Sorry about that. Marcus is getting on my nerves."

"What did you find out about his new girlfriend?" I asked. Might as well get in somebody else's business since it seemed everybody was in mine.

"She seems nice. I've talked to her a couple of

times. I've run into her in the hallway. The only thing is—she rarely looks you in the eyes."

"Maybe she's shy."

"Marcus seemed pissed one day when he saw us talking. He grabbed her arm and nearly pushed her into the locker."

"I guess he didn't want you telling her he was still hounding you."

"Probably. I'm so glad I don't talk to him like that anymore. I think Marcus is more like DJ than any of us first thought," Britney said.

"They are cousins so that's not hard to believe," I responded.

"Marcus has been calling me a little too much. Sometimes when I'm walking to class, I feel as if someone is watching me. Every single time it happens, I look around and he's there."

"Wow. Marcus is crazy. Girl, you better be careful."

"He's harmless. He's probably still torn about me breaking up with him last year." Britney sounded like she was trying to convince herself of this more than me.

I responded, "That was a year ago. He should be over it by now."

"You know the dude I went to the homecoming dance with, Luther?" Britney asked.

Since she wanted to change the subject, I obliged. "What's up with him?" I asked.

"He's a jerk too. He keeps trying to pressure me to have sex with him. He doesn't understand that I want to wait. He had the nerve to call me a B."

I said, "I don't know what's up with the guys. Cecil told me Cameron's only talking to Lauren because she's willing to sleep with him and he knows I'm one of the good girls."

"At least you know so you can stop wasting your energy on him," Britney said.

I didn't agree with Britney. I felt like Cameron and I could still be good together, but not just in that way. If he was still my boyfriend when I went to college, then yes, maybe; but as long as we were in high school, my virginity would stay intact.

Britney clicked over to her other line. She came back on the line. "That's Jas. She's mad because you're mad. You two never quit."

"We have that love-hate relationship going on."

"According to Dr. Phil, your friendship is toxic. I should disown both of you and get me a new set of friends," Britney said.

"You know you love the drama as much as Jasmine loves being a drama queen."

"I heard that," Jasmine said. I wasn't aware she was on the line.

"Bri," I yelled.

"Now kiss and make up so I can get me some sleep," Britney said.

Jasmine reluctantly said, "I'm sorry I didn't get your permission first before giving Cecil your number."

I remained quiet. Britney said, "Sierra, your turn."

I mumbled, "And I'm sorry I went off on you."

"Now good night ladies," Britney said. With one click we were disconnected.

~ 17 ~

Sierra's Got a Man

Cecil met me at the front door of the school the next morning. Greetings were exchanged between Cecil, Britney and Jasmine. I thought he was ignoring me at first, but then he asked me, "Do you mind if I walk you to class?"

Both Cecil and I watched Jasmine to see her response. She didn't flinch. I responded, "Sure."

As we all began to walk down the hall, Jasmine said, "We'll walk ahead to give you two your privacy."

Cecil and I looked at one another. I responded, "No need to. He's just walking us to class."

"No, he's walking you. I'm walking on my own,"

Jasmine responded as she turned around and started to walk ahead of us increasing her pace with every step. Britney looked at me and shrugged her shoulders. She ran to catch up with Jasmine.

"Do you think it's working?" Cecil asked.

"She's hard to figure out," I responded.

I listened to Cecil talk about Jasmine all the way to class. Ms. Hogan wasn't there, so everyone was standing around talking. Lauren was standing behind Cameron rubbing his shoulders. Ms. Hogan walked in and the first thing she said was, "Lauren, come here."

I could tell from the expression on Lauren's face, what Ms. Hogan had to say to her wasn't nice. I smiled. That's what she got for acting like a slut.

Cameron rushed behind me in the hallway as I left to go to my other class. "Thanks for hooking me up with your boy. With his help, I'll be able to pass that next test," he said.

I responded, "No problem."

"I really would like to thank you. Maybe we . . ."

Before he could finish his statement, Lauren walked up. "You need to get your own man."

Cecil happened to walk up. "Sierra's got a man. So what's going on here?" Cecil wrapped his arm around my shoulders.

We all waited for Lauren's response. "She needs to act like it," she said, as she stormed away.

Cameron said, "You have to ignore Lauren. She has anger issues."

I said, "Among other things."

"Man, we're still on for this evening?" Cameron asked.

"Meet me in the lab as soon as school lets out," Cecil said.

Cameron walked away, leaving me and Cecil standing there by ourselves. Well, not really by ourselves, since the hallway was packed with other students trying to make it to class before the tardy bell rang.

We talked as Cecil walked with me in the direction of my next class. "I had that situation under control Mister Sierra's got a Man."

"Oh, I'm sure you did. Did you see how Cameron looked when I put my arm around you?" he asked.

I did notice the surprised look on his face. "He did seem shocked."

"So what do you say? Why don't we fake it? Cameron and Jasmine both might come to their senses."

The tardy bell rang. Fortunately, I was standing right outside my class. "I'll let you know."

"Think about it," he said, before rushing across the hall to his class.

The rest of my morning went by fast. Britney and Jasmine were huddled up at our table in the lunchroom by the time I got there. I grabbed a tuna sandwich and a bowl of fruit and slid into the chair.

"You didn't waste any time did you?" Jasmine asked.

While unwrapping my sandwich, I said, "What are you talking about?"

Britney said, "Folks are talking about the scene between you and Lauren."

Jasmine added, "Seems like your knight in shining armor came to your rescue. Right before Lauren got a chance to whoop that butt."

I threw my sandwich down on the plate. "First of all, you're supposed to be my girl, but you act like you're happy to report a false rumor like that. Second of all, I was handling the situation long before Cecil walked up on the scene. Third of all . . ."

"Calm down," Britney said.

Several people were looking in our direction. I didn't realize at first that my voice had escalated. I lowered my voice. "Jas, for someone who doesn't want Cecil, you sure act like you do."

"I don't want him. But you're a diva and you're not supposed to be acting like that in public."

"People throw around the word diva too much anyway and you're always ready to throw the first punch. I don't know why you're trying to give me advice anyway."

"Ladies. It seems I'm always playing referee," Britney said.

"Yeah it does. Maybe we need a break," I said, as I picked up my tray and left the table.

I saw Cecil sitting by himself. I placed my tray on the table. "Do you mind?" I asked.

"No, of course not. Have a seat," Cecil said.

I glanced over where Britney and Jasmine were seated. Jasmine would turn her head every time she noticed me looking. "Tell me again why I am friends with them."

"Even the best of friends have disagreements," Cecil said.

I shrugged my shoulders. "I guess."

"I know so. My best friend is mad at me now because I won't let him borrow my video game I just got."

"That's stupid."

"Yes, that's what I think too. But my friend doesn't think so. I'll let him cool down and then all will be well again."

Cecil had a point. I would let things cool down some before talking to my BFFs.

~ 18 ~
The Cover Up

That day after school, I rushed out of my last period class so I could make it outside without having to see Britney or Jasmine. Maria's timing was perfect. She was already parked outside. I had to tap on the window to get her attention because she seemed engrossed in her phone conversation and hadn't noticed me walk up. I wasn't trying to be nosy, but it sounded like she was on the phone with my dad.

She confirmed it, when I heard her say, "Jorge, I'm sorry. It won't happen again."

Once she ended the call, she said, "When we get home, go straight to your room. Your dad's tripping about money again."

What now? I said to myself. "Was that my dad you were talking to?"

"Yes and he's mad that I went over budget on your homecoming gown."

"No we didn't," I said.

"Yes, we did. Remember, the dress was a thousand dollars."

"No, it was half of that because we got it off the fifty percent off rack."

"The original price was a thousand dollars. If your father asks you that, that's what you tell him," she said.

"The tag said one thousand but it rang up five hundred."

"Look Missy. I'm always going to bat with your father about things you want to do. Do you know he really didn't want you to be a Dancing Diamond?"

I wondered if she was telling the truth. She continued to talk. "I was the one who convinced him you needed to have an extracurricular activity. So telling him the dress cost a thousand dollars is not asking you too much."

Maria had a point; although I didn't like the way she went about demanding that I lie to my dad because of her shopping habits. My dad, who was rarely at home when I got there from school, confronted me as soon as I walked through the door. "I need to talk to you in private," he said, ignoring Maria.

"I'll be cooking dinner if either one of you need me," she said.

I followed my dad into the living room. I threw my backpack down on the floor near the couch.

"You know I would give you my last dollar just to see that beautiful smile of yours right?" my dad asked.

"I know Daddy."

"I've talked to the entire family about us having to tighten up in some areas, with shopping for unnecessary things being one of them right?"

"Yes, but I didn't have a dress appropriate for the homecoming dance."

"I know that and I'm not upset about that, not at all."

"What I want to know from you, because Maria doesn't seem to be able to tell me the truth, is could you have found any other dress cheaper?"

Whew. I felt relieved. I wouldn't have to lie to

him after all. "I'm not sure about cheaper but that's the only dress the store had that fit me perfectly."

"You haven't been ordering anything off the internet have you?"

"No sir. Actually, I have been spending so much time studying and practicing dance routines I haven't done much shopping lately."

"Good. Let's keep it that way."

I was really worried about our finances. "Dad, if I ask you something will you be honest with me?"

"As honest as I can be," he responded.

"Are we broke?"

He laughed. "Dear, we're far from broke. I'm doing my best to make sure we never are. That's why I need you, your mom, and brother to help me out. I know you're accustomed to getting whatever you want. I promise you, for the most part, you will continue to get those things. For now, I just want to make sure we can continue to live a lifestyle that we've all got accustomed to. I don't ever want you or Zion to experience not having a roof over your head or not having any food to eat. Not like I had to when I was a little boy."

I felt bad whenever he talked about the childhood he had. His mother and father both died when he was young. He was sent from orphanage to orphanage until, one day he was adopted into a family who seemed to care about him. That didn't happen until he was about Zion's age. My dad had lived a rough life. I removed the debit card out of my purse. I handed it to him. He handed it back. "You can keep this because you never know when you'll need it."

"But Dad, I know in the past I've used it when I wasn't supposed to. I just wanted to assure you that I had your back."

"Good because I need you to help me watch Maria. Maria has gotten out of control when it comes to spending money."

I wanted to say good luck with that. Instead I said, "She's not going to listen to me."

"Oh she will. Trust me."

"Maria does what she wants to do."

"Oh, and another thing. I noticed lately you've stopped calling her mom. What's going on that I need to know about?"

This was the moment of truth. I could reveal to him more of Maria's deceitfulness or I could continue to cover up Maria's transgressions. *What should I do? Lord, forgive me*, I said to myself right before saying, "Lately, she seems to treat Zion better than me."

"Oh really now. Why didn't you say something earlier?" he asked, as he stood up to go confront Maria.

"Because I didn't want to cause problems between the two of you," I lied.

~ 19 ~

So Much Drama in the Air

I avoided Maria last night, but had no choice but to face her this morning. She smiled around my dad, but as soon as we were in the car, she went off. "I don't appreciate you lying to your dad about Zion."

"It was either that or tell him about your shopping." I knew that would shut her up.

She turned up the volume to the Tom Joyner Morning Show. I laughed louder than usual at some of the jokes just to annoy Maria. She held on to the steering wheel so tight, I thought she was going to break a nail.

"See you later. We have practice today so Brenda will be dropping me off," I said.

"Bye," she responded sharply.

I left one set of drama and walked right into another set of drama. Britney and Jasmine barely opened up their mouths to speak. "Be like that," I said, as I left them and walked towards homeroom.

I made a point of not looking up when Britney and Jasmine walked in the room. After class, Jasmine slipped me a note. I took it but kept walking. I read it while I was supposed to be reading a chapter from my science book. I placed the note back in my backpack. I really don't see how I had changed. To me, I was the same Sierra. Britney and Jasmine were just used to being in the spotlight. Now that I was getting more attention, neither one of them could handle it. I decided to be the bigger person. When I saw them at lunch, I pretended like all was well. Lately, I had been doing a lot of pretending.

"I'm surprised you're not sitting with your boyfriend again today," Jasmine said.

I took a few deep breaths. I would not let Jasmine pull me into her world of drama. I responded,

"For the record, Cecil's not my boyfriend. If you act right, he could be yours."

"Well, he really likes you. I can tell by the way he looks at you."

Britney said, "Jas, that's enough."

I said, "What isn't to like? From what I understand, I have it going on."

"Who told you that?" Jasmine leaned back in her chair and asked.

"A few guys, including Cecil."

Umph. I think I hit a nerve there. Jasmine opened her mouth to say something but stopped after she looked at Britney.

"The color of hater-aid doesn't look good on you Jas," I said.

Jasmine laughed. "Please. I will never ever be jealous of another girl."

"Chill out, please," Britney said, annoyed with our back and forth banter.

The drama in the air was so thick you could cut it with a knife. We barely said anything else to each other during the rest of our lunch. It's like we couldn't wait to go our separate ways.

Cecil was waiting for me outside of my fifth period class. "I saw Jasmine earlier. She gave me a straight up attitude so I think it's working."

"I don't mean to burst your bubble, but her attitude has nothing to do with you. We got into it again."

"Oh," was all Cecil could say. "Well, what are you doing after school?"

"I got dance practice. What about you?"

"I'm tutoring Cameron and a few other people in calculus."

"Don't work them too hard."

"I won't. Can I call you later?" he asked.

"Sure why not. According to everybody, we're talking anyway."

After dance rehearsal, Britney and I waited in the gym for Jasmine to finish cheerleading practice.

"Isn't that Marcus' girlfriend?" I pointed to a girl sitting on the bleachers.

"Yes. Let's go say hi," Britney said.

When we got near her, I noticed she had bruises on her face. Britney and I exchanged looks. Britney said, "We keep running into each other but I don't know your name."

"Cassie," she responded.

"I'm Britney and this is my best friend Sierra."

"Hi," I said.

"Do you mind if we sit?" Britney asked.

Cassie looked around as if she was looking for someone and waiting on them to respond for her. "I guess it'll be okay."

"I don't remember seeing you here last year," Britney said.

"I transferred from Roosevelt High."

"What grade are you in?" I asked.

"I'm in the tenth."

Britney said, "So how long have you and Marcus been talking?"

"I would rather not say," Cassie responded.

"No biggie. I just asked," Britney said.

"There goes my favorite girl," Marcus said, as he walked up the bleachers and took a seat next to Cassie. I doubt he meant Cassie was his favorite girl since he was looking at Britney when he said it.

"What's up ladies?" he asked.

"Nothing much," Britney responded. "We were just keeping Cassie company until you came."

"I'm here now, so you can go."

"Excuse me," Britney said.

"I'm not trying to be rude but there's some stuff me and Cassie need to talk about," Marcus said. "In private if you don't mind." He looked at Britney and then at me.

I grabbed Britney's arm. "Come on girl, let's go. Cassie, it was nice meeting you."

She didn't look at us at all once Marcus came to sit by her.

"She was opening up until Marcus brought his behind over there," I said.

"I wonder how she got those bruises." Britney said.

"Me too. I had hoped you would ask."

"I would have but Marcus walked up too quick."

"I wonder if her parents are abusing her. Maybe we should tell one of our teachers," I said.

Britney said, "I'll talk to my mom about it and see what we should do."

"Sometimes we don't realize how lucky we are," I said.

"No, you mean how blessed," Britney said, correcting me.

I had a funny feeling that Marcus was behind those bruises. Britney needed to be careful around Marcus. Before exiting the door, I turned around in Marcus and Cassie's direction and Marcus was staring back, causing a chill to go up and down my spine.

~ 20 ~

Control

Friday after school, Britney and I crashed over at Jasmine's. During the summer we had stopped our monthly get together but in light of the tension lately, Britney insisted we start it back up. Jasmine volunteered to be the first hostess. Things with Maria were a little tense so she was more than thrilled that she wouldn't have to deal with me this weekend.

While we took turns polishing each other's fingernails Britney said, "I think Marcus is abusing Cassie."

Jasmine said, "No way. Not sweet Marcus."

"I spoke with my mom about it and from what I told her, she says it sounds like abuse."

I said, "Maybe it's her parents." Although I felt she was probably right.

"If it was, she wouldn't be so jumpy every time Marcus is around or near."

"His tone with her was forceful," I said, as I thought about what transpired in the gym earlier that week.

"I told my mom about the times I've run into them and she said it sounds like abuse. She was shocked to learn Marcus was the guy I was referring to."

"Good thing you left him alone," I said.

"Girl, please. If Marcus tried that mess with me, I would go upside his head," Britney responded.

"Maybe we could get her some help," I said.

"I think y'all need to mind your own business. Apparently she loves it, if she's letting him force her around like that," Jasmine said.

"She might feel like she has no choice. I don't ever see her hanging out with anyone," I said.

Britney told Jasmine about our last encounter with her. Jasmine sounding annoyed said, "Cassie is a fool and Brenda says you have to leave a fool to themselves."

Britney responded, "Jas, I can't believe you feel

that way. If that was one of us, what would you do?"

"Tell you what I thought about the situation and then let you make your own decision."

Britney and I said in unison, "Yeah right."

Britney remarked, "You would hound us until we saw your view."

I added, "I'm a witness."

"I don't even know this Cassie chick," Jasmine affirmed.

"I don't really know her either, but still. She needs to know she has choices," Britney replied.

I uttered, "Bri, why don't you talk to her? Let her know if she needs a friend, we're here."

Jasmine pointed at the both of us. "You're there for her. I don't know the chick and really don't want to know her if she's that weak to be letting a boy push her around like that."

Brenda, who unbeknownst to us, had been standing in the doorway listening to our conversation intervened and said, "I heard some of your conversation. Jasmine, girls, let me school you on a few things."

She walked into Jasmine's room and took a seat. Brenda said, "It's not hard to get caught up in an abusive situation. People who you think wouldn't be involved in one, end up in them."

"But how? If a guy talks crazy to you—nip it then. Walk away," Jasmine said.

"Easier said than done. Most abusers don't come off as abusers. They start off as if they really care about the girl. The abuser starts playing with the girl's mind. He claims to love her more than everyone else," Brenda said.

We had all stopped whatever we were doing and gave Brenda our full attention. "I never would have thought Marcus was the type," Jasmine said.

"Most abusers are able to hide that side of themselves from others," Brenda said.

"Jas thinks we shouldn't say anything, but I think someone needs to try to help Cassie," Britney said.

Brenda said, "You can try but don't be disappointed if she doesn't look too kindly on you interfering."

"She should be thrilled that someone's trying to help her," I said.

"Think about it. She doesn't know you all. For all she knows, you could be reporting back to Marcus. If Marcus is doing what y'all think he's doing to her, in her mind, it'll only make things worse."

"I hadn't thought about that," I said.

Jasmine moved around on the bed. "I still think we should mind our own business. It might not even be what we think it is."

Brenda said, "But it could be. Women need to watch out for other women. That's what's wrong with the world now. Folks no longer look out for each other."

Ironically, the first song we heard on the radio, when Jasmine turned it on was "Control."

Jasmine flipped the station. "You two do what you want to. I'm staying out of it."

Britney said, "I'll talk to her. In fact, I'll do better than that. I'll talk to Marcus."

I said, "Wait. I don't think that's a good idea."

"Marcus is not going to do anything to me," Britney responded. She dialed Marcus' number and put him on speaker phone. "Y'all be quiet," she said.

Marcus answered. "I knew you would come to your senses and want me back."

Britney laughed. "I don't think so Marcus. Our time is a thing of the past."

"Just say the word and I'll get rid of my girlfriend," he said.

"Speaking of your girlfriend, what's with her?" Britney asked.

"What do you mean?" he asked, sounding defensive.

"She seems cool when you're not around and as soon as you show up, she clams up," Britney said.

"I don't know. She acts crazy like that sometimes," Marcus responded.

I looked at Britney and mouthed the words, "Yeah right."

"I'm real disappointed in you," Britney said.

"We're not together anymore so why do you care?" he asked.

"I don't," she responded.

"Oh, you're going to be mine again. Just watch and see," he said.

Britney said, "This conversation is over. And Marcus, please lose my number and stop calling me and texting me."

"You know you like it. Stop fronting."

"Bye Marcus."

"It'll never be bye for us," he said.

"Just hang the phone up," Jasmine said, not caring if Marcus heard her or not.

Britney did as instructed. I said, "He is crazy. I can't stand him or his trifling cousin DJ."

"Marcus is not as bad as DJ," Britney said.

Jasmine interrupted her. "I can't believe you're defending him after he said what he said."

"I'm just saying. I know Marcus better than you two. He could never be as bad as DJ."

It was clear Britney was living in denial. We stopped talking about Marcus and started talking about clothes, a topic we could all agree upon.

~ 21 ~

To Shop or Not To Shop

I dreamt Marcus was chasing me down the school hallway after I beat him up for beating up his girlfriend. I was so happy that Jasmine shook me to wake me up the next morning. Jasmine said, "Girl, you're sweating like you were running a marathon."

"I was dreaming," I responded.

"Brenda's dropping us off at the mall, so we best get up and get ready because you know once she's ready to go, she's ready to go," Jasmine said. "Bri is already in the shower so you can go to the bathroom down the hall."

Wiping the sleep from my eyes, I slowly got out of bed and retrieved a few items out of my overnight bag that I kept at Jasmine's. "I don't know what I want to wear," I said, as I took out two different outfits.

"I'm wearing jeans," Jasmine said.

"Then I'll wear mine too," I said, as I put my skirt back in the bag.

Two hours later Brenda was dropping us off at the Galleria. Temptation was all around me as we went from store to store. Jasmine and Britney splurged on several outfits. I tried on some outfits and pretended as if I didn't like them well enough to purchase them. Britney said, "I'll get this one if you really want it."

I thought about the conversation I had with my dad. Even if I let Britney purchase it for me, he wouldn't be happy to learn about it. "That's okay. I don't like it that much."

"I'll get it," Jasmine said, throwing it on the counter with her items as she pulled out her credit card.

The sales clerk said, "May I see your ID?"

"Why do you need to see my ID? I shop here all of the time."

"There's a fraud alert on this card. Unless you

show me your ID all of this," she pointed to the items on the counter, "will not be leaving this store."

I really hated this sales clerk's attitude. I said, "Jasmine, get your card. Let's go to another store."

Jasmine didn't move. "No. I know what it is. She thinks we can't afford this stuff and we stole the card. Well, I don't have to steal. My dad is . . ."

Britney cut her off. "Can she have her card back please and we'll be on our way."

"I'm afraid I can't do that unless she shows me an ID."

Jasmine pulled out her wallet, removed her ID and threw it on the counter. "Satisfied? Now give me back my credit card and let me see a manager."

"Ms. McNeil, I apologize."

An older woman dressed immaculately walked over. "Is there a problem here?"

Jasmine whispered to us. "Watch this. I've seen my mom do this many times." She turned and faced the woman who we assumed was the manager. "Yes. Your employee has been giving us a hard time just because she thought we couldn't afford to buy this stuff."

"Karen, what are they talking about?"

We stood and waited and watched Karen explain herself to her manager. The manager addressed us.

"Young ladies, I apologize for this. For your problem, if you still make this purchase, I will give you ten percent off."

The light in Jasmine's eyes lit up. "Sierra, you still want that outfit? Ten percent off and it was already on sale."

"Sure," I said. I couldn't resist. I made a mental note to pay her back.

We were laughing and walking towards the food court when I heard someone say, "There goes the girl who wants my man."

Jasmine said, "I know she's not talking to one of us."

Britney said, "Come on. Let's not stoop down to her level."

I said loud enough for Lauren and her friends to hear. "I didn't even know she could afford to shop in the Galleria."

"Oh no you didn't. I ought to snatch that weave out of your head," Lauren said.

I ignored Britney's suggestion and so did Jasmine. We both stopped and turned around to face Lauren. I ran my hand through my hair before flipping it over one of my shoulders. "A track never sees this scalp. Too bad you can't say that."

Jasmine held up her bags. "Now, if you don't mind, we have more shopping to do."

Jasmine said, as we got closer to where Britney was standing, "They sure got quiet."

"Who cares? Little does she know the only reason why Cameron is with her is because she's giving it up," I said.

We got us a quick bite to eat at the food court before heading to another store. We stopped at the Sephora store to see if they had any new flavors of lip gloss. I didn't hesitate to use my card to purchase a few tubes of lip gloss. I hadn't spent any of my allowance money in a long time, so I didn't feel guilty since the lip gloss was a small purchase.

"That's Brenda," Jasmine said, after hanging up her phone.

"I'm ready because this not being able to shop is straight up torture," I confessed.

"I told you I got you," Britney said.

"But I would still have to explain where I got the stuff from. My dad would have a fit. I can sneak in the one outfit Jas got me but coming home with bags of stuff, oh no. Maria doing it in our household is enough."

"Maria sounds like a shopaholic," Jasmine said.

Britney responded, "It takes one to know one."

It felt good sharing a laugh with my friends.

~ 22 ~

Pound for Pound

"Sierra, I need to talk to you for a moment," Ms. Vernon said, after dance rehearsal.

"Bri, I'll catch up with you later," I said, before walking over to where Ms. Vernon stood.

"I've noticed you've lost a lot of weight recently."

"Yes ma'am."

"You seemed a little light-headed earlier so I wanted to make sure you weren't starving yourself," she came out and said.

"No ma'am. I think it was because I hadn't drunk any water today."

Ms. Vernon said, "I know there's a lot of pressure to be thin; but your main concern should be your health."

"But last year I was told I should lose some weight."

"Maybe you needed to last year, but your weight is fine for your height."

I listened to Ms. Vernon and although I was glad she felt I was fine for the dance team, I still felt like I could stand to lose a few more pounds. Especially since it seemed the boy that I liked was into the skinny girls.

"What did Ms. Vernon want?" Britney asked when I caught up with her about ten minutes later.

"She wanted to talk about my weight."

"You look fine to me," Britney said, as we headed outside to see if Maria was there.

I said, "She agreed. She was concerned about me not eating."

"You have lost a lot of weight," Britney said.

"But I'm eating. I just don't eat as much as I used to," I said.

Maria wasn't in the best of moods when we got to the car. Her and my dad must have gotten into another argument. I talked to Britney until we dropped her off at home. We rode home in silence. I rushed upstairs once we got home.

"Can you help me with my homework?" Zion asked.

"What you got?" I asked, as I moved over on my bed to give him room to sit down.

He placed his spelling book in front of me. "I need to know how to use each one of these in a sentence."

"Why can't Maria help you?" I asked.

"She's busy."

"Too busy to help you with your homework?" *Something really was going on.*

By the time I helped Zion with his homework, it was time for dinner. "Sierra, I wouldn't put too many potatoes on my plate if I were you," Maria said.

I dropped the spoon and some potatoes splashed. My dad said, "Get as much as you want. Maria, we've had this conversation before. Let's not do a repeat."

"But . . ." she said.

"Sierra has lost enough weight. If she loses anymore, she'll be anorexic."

"I'm just trying to look after your daughter's welfare," Maria responded.

My dad said, "Stop trying to put your insecurities with your weight off on my daughter."

Maria knew when to challenge my dad and when not to. It was obvious this was one of those times for her to retreat. She realized it too because she didn't say anything else about how much food I was piling on my plate.

Zion was the center of attention throughout the course of the dinner. I didn't say much. I noticed how my dad went out of his way to ignore Maria's comments. All wasn't well in the Sanchez household.

"Sierra, I'm not feeling well, so I need you to wash dishes tonight," Maria said, once we were all through eating.

I sure hated not having a live in maid. I never had to wash dishes before. Well, I did on occasion, but that was only because my dad insisted I know how to do work around the house. He didn't want me to be a spoiled brat, like some people he knew, namely Jasmine.

After washing dishes, I finished my homework. I went online to check out some of the gossip blogs. An advertisement for some diet pills popped up. I contemplated on whether or not I should click on it. It wouldn't hurt anything, so I did. The web page redirected me from the gossip blog to a page where the people had claims of losing twenty to a hundred pounds in a short period of time.

I thought about my quest to lose a few more pounds. If I got the diet pills, I could still eat the same amount I was eating and all would be well in my world. The price was just right. I clicked on the ordering form and placed an order for a thirty day supply. It would have been cheaper to order a ninety day supply so I decided to change my order before hitting the final submit button.

I closed my eyes and imagined myself several sizes smaller. *Cameron no longer went out with Lauren. He went out of his way to be with me. In fact, all the guys were beating each other up to get near me.*

The phone ringing broke me out of my daydream. "I hope this isn't a bad time," Cecil said, from the other end of the phone.

"It was, but what do you want," I said, as I logged off the computer.

"I just wanted to talk. See how you were doing. See if you needed to talk," he responded.

"Nope. I'm fine."

"You don't sound fine."

"Cecil, go bother someone else okay," I said, as I hung up the phone.

Oh my goodness. I'm acting just like Jasmine.

~ 23 ~

Hidden Treasures

M y package came just in time for the Sadie Hawkins dance. I hid the contents of the box under my bed and placed a few pills in my backpack so I could take them before meals as instructed. I really wished I could talk to Britney or Jasmine about this, but since neither one of them ever had a weight issue, I didn't feel like I could. Britney would understand, but Jasmine would be typical Jasmine and flaunt the fact that she didn't have to diet to maintain a healthy weight.

I saw Cecil talking with a group of kids. I was rude the last time I talked to him so I made it a point to apologize. "Apology accepted," he responded. "I understand you're under a lot of stress."

"That still doesn't excuse my behavior," I said.

He shrugged his shoulders. "Want to grab something to eat after the game Friday," he said.

"I'll have to pass. My dad's picking us up and he's not at the stage where he's going to let me go out with a guy." I reached into my backpack looking for some gum. I held on to the tissue holding my pills as I searched.

"Tell him, I'm just a friend."

I laughed. "You don't know my dad. He would ask you a million and one questions and then tell you that his daughter is too young to date."

"I'm sure he's not that bad," Cecil said.

"Try it and see. I dare you," I said. The grip I had on the tissue loosened and the diet pills accidentally fell on the floor.

Cecil bent down and picked it up. He observed the pills. "We really need to talk."

I snatched the pills out of his hand. "These are diet pills, nothing more."

"Sierra, you don't need those pills. You look just fine just the way you are," he said.

"Mind your own business," I said, as I stuffed the tissue with the pills back in my backpack.

"I've heard bad things about those types of pills."

"Well, keep the information to yourself."

Not wanting to hear what else Cecil had to say, I rushed through the crowd to my next class. I snuck and took the pills right before going into the lunch room. My head felt lightheaded but that was probably because I wasn't drinking enough water.

In the middle of lunch, Jasmine said, "Your boyfriend keeps looking this way."

"Cameron's too busy talking to Lauren to look this way."

"I'm talking about Cecil."

Cecil waved when I looked in his direction. I waved back. "I keep telling you nothing's happening with Cecil."

"You two do make a cute couple," Britney said.

"I think Jas and Cecil are cuter together," I responded.

"I didn't want to tell y'all yet because it's not official, but you guys know Trevon right?" Jasmine said.

"Tre's only the cutest boy in the junior class," Britney said.

"I've been talking to him a lot lately and he wants me to be his girlfriend."

Trevon Wright had girls of all ages drooling over him. I even noticed some of the teachers making comments. It was rumored that his parents owned a chewing gum factory. Who would have ever thought you could get rich off of chewing gum.

"You're always up in somebody else's business, but you've been hush-hush about this," I stated.

"I didn't want to jinx it. So now are we clear about my stance on Cecil. If you want him, go for it. Trevon is who I want."

I thought about what Jasmine said; however I wanted Cameron to show more interest in me. Once I lost a few more pounds, he would forget Lauren. He would be so happy to be with me, it wouldn't bother him that I wanted to wait to have sex. Yes, Cameron won't know what hit him when I lose twenty more pounds.

"Earth to Sierra," Britney said several times.

"What did you say?" I asked.

"Who are you asking to the Sadie Hawkins dance this year?" Britney repeated.

"I hadn't decided. I want to ask Cameron, but I'm not sure."

Jasmine said, "Forget Cameron. Ask somebody else."

"I don't want to forget Cameron. I know he's been kicking it with Lauren, but according to Cecil, it's not that serious."

Britney said, "Do you really want a boy who is only with a girl for her body?"

Good question. I didn't have an answer for that, especially since I was on a mission to lose weight so he would think my body was banging. I unzipped my back pack and took a quick glance at the other hidden treasures I had there for the next time I had a meal. I zipped it back up and continued to talk to Britney and Sierra until it was time to go to class.

Cecil tried to get my attention before leaving the lunch room, but I ignored him. "I'll call you," he yelled.

As I said earlier, now I see what Jasmine meant by Cecil being a pest.

~ 24 ~

The Clique

Lauren and her clique were standing outside of the lunchroom when we exited. We stood nearly face to face. Lauren approached me. She now stood about a foot away. "What's that noise you were saying at the mall?"

Jasmine opened her mouth to talk. I said, "I got this." I looked directly at Lauren. Since she was a few inches shorter than me, I had to look down. "I didn't stutter the first time."

"I'm so sick and tired of hearing your name. Sierra this, Sierra that. You need to stay away from my man," she said, as she had one hand on her hip and moved her neck from side to side.

"If you were secure in your relationship, then

you wouldn't be all up in my face now, would you?" I said, with confidence. My blood pressure increased as I felt the tension in my head.

Her two friends stood back with their arms crossed. Britney and Jasmine stood near me waiting to see if anything was going to jump off.

"I can tell you like leftovers, from the way you look. First you went after Tanisha's man DJ and now you're after mine."

"I can't get what can't get got," I said, not blinking an eye.

"Be warned. The next time I see you batting those long eye lashes at my man, I won't be too nice."

I don't know what came over me, but I took a few steps closer to Lauren. "If you try to lay one hand on me, I will turn your blond hair black."

Jasmine said, "You go girl."

"I suggest you get out of my face," Lauren said, as we now stood face to face.

"You don't own this hallway. Move around," I said, as I now stood with one of my hands on my hip.

One of Lauren's friends said, "Girl, it's not worth getting suspended for. Come on let's go."

Lauren backed up. "You better be glad she stopped me."

I crossed my arms. "No, you better be glad."

Lauren and her friends walked away. I released my breath. Jasmine came up to me and hugged me. "Girl, you make me so proud. You've transformed from the quiet Sierra we all know and love to a kick-butt diva."

Britney said, "It did look like you were ready to throw some blows."

"She caught me on the wrong day," I said. I was prepared to protect myself, but I really was putting up a front. I was more nervous than anything, but of course I wouldn't tell them that.

"Ladies, you need to get to class," the hall monitor said.

"See y'all later," I said.

"If I need a bodyguard, I'll text you," Jasmine teased.

I felt light-headed as I walked to class. I didn't know if it was because I was still pumped up from the confrontation with Lauren or side effects from the diet pills. Throughout the day, I replayed the events and wondered what I would have done if things had gone in another direction. My father would be mad if I messed up my perfect conduct record. I had never gotten in trouble before. Lauren brought out the worst side of me. She had

Cameron so I don't know why she felt threatened by me.

Later that night Cecil called me. I asked, "How's your tutoring sessions going with Cameron?"

"He's not the brightest," he informed me. I didn't know if he was saying that out of jealousy or he really meant Cameron wasn't smart.

"Everybody is not as smart as you," I responded. I meant it too. Cecil was one of the smartest kids I knew. I thought I was smart, but he knew way more than me.

"I'll take the compliment. What else do you think about me?" Cecil asked.

I held out my hand to count; although he couldn't see me. "Let's see. You're smart. You have a nice personality. You're kind of cute. You would be alright if you weren't such a pest. Can I think of anything else?" I teased.

"You've said enough."

"Did I hurt your feelings? I'm sorry," I said.

"No, I'm fine," he responded.

"I'm serious. I think you're all those things. I was kidding about the pest part though."

"Wow. Thanks. I think."

"Let me tell you what happened earlier after lunch," I said, needing someone unbiased to talk to about the situation. I repeated the chain of events. "Can you believe she approached me like that?"

"Lauren thinks you're my girlfriend so she called me trying to cause problems between us. She slipped me a note alerting me to your pursuit of Cameron."

"Interesting. Well, if we were really going together, that would be messed up."

"It wouldn't faze me because if you ever gave me a chance to be your boyfriend, you wouldn't want to be with another guy. I would know Lauren was lying," Cecil responded.

"Oh really now. How is that?" I asked out of curiosity. Cecil did not seem like the nerd that Jasmine portrayed.

"I am sincere in whatever I do. I don't disrespect my girl or any other girls. I don't have to pretend to be something I'm not. I'm secure in who I am." Cecil said it with conviction. He almost had me believing him.

"How many girlfriends have you had?" I asked.

"Enough," Cecil responded.

By the time our conversation ended, I was curious to know more about Cecil; although thoughts of Cameron lingered in the back of my mind.

~ 25 ~

Sadie Hawkins

The Sadie Hawkins dance was getting near and I still hadn't asked a guy out. I noticed Cameron standing by himself so I walked up to him. "Can I talk to you for a minute?" I asked.

"What's up Sierra?" he asked,

"Are you and Lauren together or is she making more out of it than what it is?" I asked.

"We're just kicking it," he responded.

From what Jasmine's sister Brenda said about "kicking it," that meant he was fair game. I had lost ten pounds by taking those diet pills and I hoped he could tell. "Where's your phone?" I asked.

He handed it to me. I punched in my ten digit number. "Call me tonight." I walked away feeling confident. I made sure I twisted my hips as I went to my next class. The rest of the day could not go by fast enough for me. While Brenda drove me home, I told Jasmine "I gave Cameron my number."

"Forget Cameron."

"You don't know that to say that," I said.

"I know enough. He's nothing like Tre," Jasmine said.

"What do you know about Tre?" I asked.

"Who is Tre?" Brenda asked as she zoomed through traffic.

"I know more than you know about Cameron. I can do a Google search on Tre's family. You can't say the same about Cameron," Jasmine said.

"So what if he doesn't come from a family with money? Money isn't everything."

"Hold up, this is where I need to interrupt you," Brenda said. "Money might not be everything, but it does matter."

I started singing the "Gold-digger" lyrics to an old Kanye West song. Brenda said, "You girls need to stop worrying about these knucklehead boys and concentrate on your books."

"Like you did," Jasmine said.

Brenda responded, "Oh you got jokes."

Jasmine had a love and hate type relationship

with her older sister. Brenda was in college and from what Jasmine told us, would get into a heap of trouble when she was in high school because she was always trying to sneak out to hang out with friends.

Jasmine said, "Drop me off at Dad's. I'm having dinner with him."

"I wished you would have told me before I drove all the way on this side of Plano," Brenda responded.

"Forget it. I'll just have him come pick me up from Sierra's."

"No. I'll drop you off. I need to ask him something anyway."

Jasmine said, "I think I'm beginning to agree with Dad. You only talk to him when you want some money."

"Just because he's divorcing mom and moved doesn't mean things are going to change in that department. As our mom says, he's the man and he needs to take care of his kids."

"But you're grown," Jasmine said.

"I'm a struggling college student who is under twenty-one," Brenda said, as if she was reciting statistics during a school lecture.

"You can let me off here," I said. I was tired of hearing about their family drama. I had enough family drama of my own to deal with and the main culprit was outside now watering the flowers.

Maria waved and Brenda and Jasmine waved back. "See you tomorrow," Jasmine said, as she let me out of the back seat of the Mustang.

"Later gators," I said, as I walked up the walkway to the house.

"How was school?" Maria asked, as she wiped some of the sweat from her forehead.

"It was alright."

"Zion got sick earlier today, so he's upstairs sleeping. Check on him for me," she said, as she continued to work in the flowerbed.

I mumbled to myself, "If you are so concerned, why aren't you checking on him?"

"What did you say dear?" she asked, as I headed to the front door.

"Nothing," I responded.

I peeped through Zion's bedroom door. He was curled up under the covers in his bed. I pulled the door back a little to keep some of the light from the hallway out of his room. I quietly walked across the hall to my room. I decided to leave my door open just in case he woke up and needed something. I gave Zion a hard time because he was my younger brother but I loved him.

I snuck and took two diet pills before dinner. Zion's absence at the dinner table was felt as I was forced to listen to Maria talk about nothing. My dad didn't seem too thrilled at what she had to say either. We both looked relieved when dinner was over and we could all leave the dinner table to go our separate ways. The whole time we were eating, my mind was on what Jasmine said. *Maybe, I should forget Cameron.*

Later on I was relaxing and watching television when my phone rang. "What are you doing?" a husky voice asked from the other end.

I wasn't familiar with the number so I asked, "It depends on who this is."

"Sierra, it's me Cameron."

He sounded good over the phone. "I'm flipping stations. Nothing is on I really want to see."

"Watch me," he said. "I got my webcam hooked up so log on and we can talk."

After the situation that happened earlier this year with Jasmine and the internet predator, my parents disabled certain features on the computer. "I wouldn't be able to view it." I didn't want to go into details so I just said, "There's something wrong with the video."

"So why did you finally give me your number?" he asked.

"Because I have a question to ask you and I don't want any interruptions."

"You have my full attention," he assured me.

"Would you like to go to the Sadie Hawkins dance with me?" I asked, releasing my breath at the same time.

"I would go but I promised someone else I would go with them," Cameron replied.

"I should have known," I blurted.

"Aww Sierra. It's not even like that," he said.

"Well, that's all I wanted. You can delete my number now," I said.

"Don't let that one day stop us from getting to know each other better," Cameron said.

He had a point. It was just a dance. "What do you want to know?" I asked. I curled my legs up under me as I sat on the bed.

"Everything."

"No one can know everything about a person."

"What's your favorite color?" he asked.

"Red is one of them," I responded.

"What about your favorite pop?" he asked.

"I'm a Fanta girl. Any flavor will do," I responded.

"I'll have to remember that for our first date," Cameron said.

My dad knocked on the door. I was supposed to be in bed. I said, "Got to go." Without waiting on Cameron to respond, I flipped the phone off, threw it under my covers and yelled, "Come in."

My dad walked in and turned off the light. "I know you were on the phone. Catch you again after hours and your phone privileges will be revoked. Understood?"

"Yes, Sir." I was talking low and used my cell phone not the house phone so I don't know how he knew I was on the phone. Parents seemed to have super sensitive ears at times.

~ 26 ~

My Back Up

I admitted to Britney and Jasmine the next day my disappointment that Cameron had already been asked to the dance. Britney asked Luther to go with her and Jasmine bragged about going with Tre. "This dance will determine whether or not we will go to the next level," Jasmine said.

I hope she didn't mean what I thought she meant. We had all promised and swore we would not have sex until after we graduated from high school—even if we didn't wait for marriage. My facial expression must have showed what I was thinking because without me having to ask, Jasmine added, "I'm not talking about sex. I'm talking about seeing one another exclusively. You know there are a lot of girls who want him, but he told me he's not feeling them at all."

Britney said, "Luther is cool but I don't see myself wanting to date him exclusively."

Jasmine said, "Well his friends think you two are going together. His boy Corey was telling me that the other day."

"I don't know what Luther is telling those guys but I'm not even trying to go there with him."

"Maybe you should have asked someone else to the dance then," I said.

"Okay, I lied. I do like him. He just has too many issues," Britney confessed.

"Like what?" I asked.

"The girls. His phone rings off the hook. It's hard to trust him."

"He's a jock so that comes with the territory," Jasmine said.

"I might not be cut out to be a baller's girlfriend," Britney said.

"Once again it looks like I won't have a date to a school dance," I said.

Jasmine said, "As much as I hate to admit it Sierra, you have no excuses not getting a date. Look at you. You've lost even more weight since school started."

"You sure have. If you don't stop losing, you're going to be paper thin like that Lauren girl," Britney said.

Little did Britney know that I wished I was as small as Lauren. "I don't eat much at dinner. You know how Maria is when it comes to food." I didn't disclose to them about the diet pills I had been taking. They made me lightheaded, but they were working.

"Well if you want to go to the dance and are just shy about asking a guy, just ask Cecil. I'm sure he'll go with you," Jasmine said.

"If you don't want to go with him, why do you keep trying to push Cecil off on me?" I asked.

"He's more your type than mine," Jasmine responded.

I looked at her with a frown on my face. She continued to say, "He's a brainiac and you're smart too."

Jasmine tried to clean up her last statement but I knew she was trying to take a quick jab at me. I let her slide this time.

Britney said, "My mom told me every girl should have a back up. Look at Cecil as your back up. If you don't ask anyone else, ask him."

"I'll think about it," I said, as I downed the rest of my food.

I didn't have any other potential prospects I could think of, so later that night I did something I had not originally planned to do. I called Cecil. "Would you like to go to the Sadie Hawkins dance with me?" I asked, without doing any of the small talk.

"It depends."

Oh no he didn't. He should be glad someone asked him.

"Was I your first choice?" Cecil asked.

Why did he care? I'm not his first choice. "Does it matter? Either you want to go or not," I said.

"I'll go but don't tell me on the day of the dance that you want to go with someone else," he said.

"Cecil, that would be so cruel. I would never do that to you or anyone else."

"It's happened to me before and I'm just making sure I'm who you want to go with before committing."

"Yes, Cecil. You are who I want to go with."

I guess boys also dealt with insecurities because Cecil seemed to have several. Jasmine and some other girls must have really messed him over. I felt sorry for him. I would make more of a conscious effort to be nicer to him; even if he did get on my nerves sometimes.

I got Britney and Jasmine both on the line. "Okay, I'm going. I asked Cecil."

"Good. Now we can go shopping for a new dress," Jasmine said.

"You two can go shopping. I doubt if my dad will let me buy a new dress since he thinks my home-coming gown cost a thousand after telling Maria not to go over five hundred," I said.

"I thought it was on sale," Jasmine said.

"It was, but Maria lied. She makes me so mad sometimes."

"If it was me, I would tell my dad," Jasmine said.

"Maria can be worrisome but my dad loves her," I said.

"What will you wear? You can't be seen in last year's dress," Britney said.

"I'll think of something," I said, as I got off the phone with them. I went from being excited about the dance to depressed because I wouldn't be able to buy a new dress. Then again, I thought about it. I could charge it to the credit card my dad gave me and then pay it off when he gave me my allowance later in the month.

I fumbled in my purse to make sure I had it in my wallet. I called Britney and Jasmine separately to let them know I would be going shopping with them. "Every girl should have a back up," I said, as I waved the credit card back and forth in the air.

~ 27 ~

The Twilight Zone

Maria was back in my good graces when she covered for me with my dad the night of the Sadie Hawkins dance. "I wished you would have told me and I could have gotten you a new dress," Maria said as she dropped me off at Jasmine's house.

"I just pulled one out of my closet," I said, as I retrieved the garment bag from the backseat.

"Well let me see what you're wearing," Maria said.

"I'm already running late. I'll make sure I take plenty of pictures," I said, as I said my good-byes and closed the door. *Whew that was close. I got on her about shopping behind my dad's back and here I am doing the same thing.*

I really was running late. Britney and Jasmine were already dressed when I arrived. I rushed up the stairs and changed into my form fitting, red, knee length, off the shoulder dress. Jasmine did my make-up and Britney did my hair.

"Looking good, chica," Jasmine said, as she admired her handiwork.

"I forgot my shoes," I said. I couldn't believe it. I was doomed.

"Got the perfect pair for you. I just have to ask Brenda if she'll let you wear them," Jasmine said.

"I'm doomed," I said out loud.

"You ask her. She'll tell you yes before she would tell me yes," Jasmine said.

I knocked on Brenda's door. "Come in," she yelled.

"Hi Bren," I said.

"Look at you. You look like a million bucks, kid."

"Thanks. I sort of have a problem though," I said, as I walked closer to where she was seated.

"Boy troubles? Have a seat and let big sister Bren school you," she said.

"Actually I need a pair of shoes. Maria, I mean, my mom, was hurrying me and I forgot to get my pair."

"Slow down. I got you. Come on, let's see what I have," Brenda said.

She led me to her walk-in closet. She had just about as many clothes as Jasmine. I saw quite a few items in her closet that I would have loved to have, but I needed to keep my attention on the shoes. She pulled out a few. "Fortunately, we wear the same size. How about these?"

She handed me a pair of silver pumps with glitters of red in them. I placed them on my feet. Brenda said, "Perfect. Check yourself out."

She closed the closet door and I admired myself in the mirror. Her shoes really complimented my dress. I gave her a big sisterly hug. "Thank you. I don't know how I will repay you."

"Just returning them without scratching them up will be payment enough."

For the second time this school year, I felt like Cinderella as I walked back across the hall to Jasmine's room. I twirled around. "So what do y'all think?" I asked.

"I hate you," Jasmine said. "Those are gorgeous. Let's trade. Bren would never know."

"I don't think so," I said, as I twirled again.

"You girls ready?" Brenda asked from the doorway.

An hour later, we stood near the door of the school auditorium, as we scanned the crowd of kids for our dates. Cecil, dressed in a black suit and red tie, walked up to us carrying a corsage. "Hi ladies." He handed me the wrist corsage. "This is for you."

"Thanks. You didn't have to."

"Yes, I did."

Jasmine left to go find her date and shortly returned. With her arm looped through Trevon's, she introduced us. "Britney, Sierra, and Cecil, this is Trevon."

"Call me Tre," he said after the introductions.

"I guess I need to text Luther. I don't see him anywhere," Britney said.

"There he is," Trevon said, pointing outside.

Luther was surrounded by several boys and girls. He spotted Britney and waved. Britney didn't look too happy. She left us to go meet him. She probably didn't want us to hear her tell him off.

"Cecil, that's a nice suit," Jasmine said.

"Thanks. You look nice too," he responded.

I cleared my throat. He said, "And so do you Sierra."

"Well thanks. After the fact," I said, as I walked away.

Cecil was fast on my heels. "You're beautiful. I hope you know that."

I pretended not to hear him. For some reason I was a little jealous of what he said to Jasmine. Something weird was going on. I shouldn't care what Cecil thought of me. I walked so fast I almost bumped into one of my teachers. "Sorry," I said, as the punch she was holding splashed on the floor barely missing Brenda's shoes.

"Let's dance," Cecil said, grabbing my arm and practically pulling me out on the dance floor.

To my surprise Cecil could dance. We danced together for several fast songs. When the deejay slowed the music down, I took that as my queue to walk off the dance floor. Cecil placed his hand on my shoulder. I turned around. He said, "Where are you going?"

"It's a slow song."

"I know," he said, as he pulled me back to him.

Cecil was several inches taller than me but with heels on, my head came to his shoulder as we twirled around the dance floor. I noticed Jasmine watching us closely. She seemed to be more interested in Cecil and me than in her date. Maybe Cecil was right after all. Maybe Jasmine really did want him and now that she sees him having a good time with me, she must be having second thoughts.

~ 28 ~

A Change of Heart

Britney and Jasmine were both spending the majority of the time with their dates. While they were doing that, Cecil kept me entertained. Not only could Cecil dance, he had a sense of humor that I hadn't noticed before tonight. Unfortunately, time was going by too fast. I had so much fun with Cecil; I didn't want the night to end.

Jasmine walked up to where we were sitting. "Brenda is right around the corner so we better be headed outside."

I looked at Cecil. "I had a good time."

He stood up and reached out his hand to help me up. "Any time you need a date, I'm your man." He kissed the back of my hand.

Jasmine rolled her eyes. "Come on. You know how she is when we're late."

Britney was already near the door. We said good-byes to a few people we saw in passing. "Did y'all have fun?" Brenda asked as soon as we pulled out from the parking lot.

"It was alright," Jasmine responded.

"I had more fun than I thought I would," I said.

Britney said, "I would have enjoyed myself if I didn't have to fight the football groupies away. The way they acted you would think Luther was in the NFL and not high school."

"I know. I'm glad I don't have to deal with that," Jasmine said.

I listened to them talk. Jasmine said, "Seems like you and Cecil were really into each other."

"We decided to have fun since we were each other's date."

"For someone who doesn't like him, you sure were dancing a little too close to him," Jasmine said.

I responded, "For someone who could care less about Cecil, why do you care?"

Brenda said, "This is like déjà vu. I thought you two learned last year about going after the same guy."

Jasmine responded, "You got it twisted. I don't like Cecil. I was just making a point to Sierra after she insisted she didn't like him. If you would have seen how they were, you would see what I meant."

"It was just a dance. Stop making such a big deal about it," I responded.

Although it was dark, I could imagine Jasmine rolling her eyes at me. She turned around in her seat and didn't say anything else to me until we got to her house. "I don't know about y'all but I'm tired," Jasmine said.

I said, "I could use a shower first, so I'll see you in the morning."

I retreated to the guest bathroom, showered and then went to bed. Brenda was the first person I saw the next morning. "Thanks again for letting me wear the shoes," I said, as I went to retrieve the shoes to give them back to their rightful owner.

"Sierra, so what's really up with you and this Cecil dude?"

Hmm. Brenda might know something I don't know. I wondered if Jasmine had confided in her about Cecil. "He's cool. A little nerdy, but folks used to say the same thing about me."

"Nerds grow up to be presidents of companies,

so don't overlook him because of that," Brenda said.

"I'll try to remember that if he ever shows interest in me. He really likes Jasmine but she won't give him the time of day."

"Oh I see. Things change. Just keep an open mind."

"Wasn't it you who said to never play second fiddle to anyone?" I asked.

Brenda responded, "I said it, but his heart can change. If it does, just keep an open mind is all I'm saying."

Jasmine's voice rang out from behind Brenda. The conversation about Cecil ceased. "I'm so hungry. I didn't eat much yesterday because I wanted to fit into my dress," Jasmine said as she and Britney walked up behind Brenda.

Speaking of dresses, Maria would be surprised to see me in a new dress when she saw the pictures. My dad wouldn't know because you could wear the same thing three times within the same week and he wouldn't notice. I slipped back into the room and retrieved two diet pills from the zipper of my purse. I cupped the water from the sink and downed the pills.

Jasmine and Britney were seated at the table eating when I entered the kitchen.

Over breakfast, Britney confessed, "I think I'm falling for Luther."

"Wow. That's deep," I said.

"I don't know what to do about the girls who are always hanging around him though. It's like me to fall for a jock when there are so many other boys out there to choose from."

"How does he feel about you?" Jasmine asked in between bites.

"Last night, he shared that he thinks he's in love."

I said, "Do you think he's only saying that so he can get you to do you know what?"

Britney seemed to be contemplating that idea. A few seconds later she responded, "I'm not sure. Maybe. He knows how I feel about it and he says he likes me so much that he's willing to wait."

Jasmine said, "I doubt if he does though."

I said, "Why do you always have to spoil the moment?"

Jasmine responded, "Think about it. He plays football. Girls are always after him. Why should he have to wait on one girl when there are plenty of other girls willing to give it to him?"

Britney bit her bottom lip. "That's what I'm worried about. I like him. He likes me. I don't want to go exclusive with him and then later end up getting hurt. I don't know if my heart could take it."

For some reason Cecil's face flashed in my thoughts. If I had a change of heart and started liking Cecil, I doubt if my heart could take another heart break either.

~ 29 ~

The Game

Normally it's either Jasmine or I facing a major dilemma, but over the next few weeks it was Britney as she contemplated whether or not to be in a relationship with Luther. Marcus was also pestering her and no matter how much Jasmine and I insisted she needed to report Marcus to her parents, she refused to do so. Being a Dancing Diamond, we got to hang out with the football jocks when we had away games. Some really were jerks, but then there were those rare ones, who seemed to have generous hearts, like Luther.

I told Britney to forget Jasmine's negative attitude towards football players. Jasmine was still pissed at Luther's friend for dissing her, so she was biased. I watched Britney and Luther's interaction from a distance on the bus ride to a football stadium in Fort Worth. He seemed to genuinely care for her. He wouldn't let the players say anything disrespectful around her.

Cecil and I sent each other text messages as I watched and waited for us to arrive. Jasmine was quiet. She seemed to be entranced with the traffic outside of our window as we rode. I whispered, "Jas, everything okay?"

She responded, "Yep. Just thinking about my dad."

"What's up with him?"

"We were supposed to get together this weekend but he has other obligations." She stressed the word "obligations."

I waited as Jasmine continued to talk. "He's met some woman and she wants him to go on a trip with her."

"Maybe you could go," I said, offering another solution.

"I said that, but they are going to Cancun. My dad doesn't feel like that's a place I should be going to; although we've been to Cancun several times as a family."

"I know it's hard seeing your dad with another woman besides your mom; but he is single."

"You wouldn't be saying that if it were your dad," Jasmine said.

"Excuse me but you must have forgotten Maria's not my real mom."

"You two seem to get along great so that's different."

"We have our moments and now is one of them, but . . ." I was not going to feed into the drama so I stopped in mid-sentence and said, "I'm sure you don't have to worry about this new woman becoming your step-mama, so stop tripping."

Jasmine didn't like my comments so she turned her head as if what was outside of the window was more important than what I had to say. I placed the earplugs to my iPod into my ears and listened to some of the songs we would be dancing to.

A few hours later, the once lively crew got on the bus feeling somber. We lost our game by two points. The ride back to school seemed to take an eternity. Maria had car pool duty so she picked us up and dropped Jasmine and Britney off at home. As soon as they were out of the car, Maria said, "I got the bill for your dress today."

Busted. I stuttered, "I was going to use my allowance to pay for it."

"Oh there will be no allowance. I paid for it so

your dad wouldn't see it. He's pinching so many pennies right now. This would have put him over the edge."

"Thanks," I said, not looking in her direction.

Maria patted the top of my hand. "That's fine. I know things have been rough between us lately. Mainly my fault, but I just wanted you to know that I have your back."

I thought about how he would have felt if he had gotten the bill instead of Maria. I now know how Maria felt when she was on a mission to hide her purchases from my dad. I didn't like the fact she tried to blackmail me, but I did understand how desperate she felt.

"Mom, we're cool," I said.

The lamp post lit up the inside of the car so I could see her smile as I stopped calling her Maria and reverted back to calling her mom. I would try to be more understanding. I hated lying to my dad but if it meant it would cause him less stress, like Maria, I would do whatever it took to handle things myself.

When we got home, I studied for my midterms. Zion informed me dinner was ready. I glanced to make sure he was not near my door and closed the door just in case he decided to return. I removed the diet pills from the box under my bed. I slipped the pills in my mouth and drowned them down with the bottled water sitting on my desk.

I glanced in the mirror and smiled because I had lost twenty pounds since taking the pills. I couldn't remember the last time I was one hundred and twenty-five pounds. My uniforms had been fitting loose so I hoped Maria or Mom could talk my dad into letting her buy me some more. I would find out tonight over dinner.

I felt a little dizzy so I held on to the rail as I walked down the stairs. I felt better once I was on level ground. Everyone was seated but me. "It's about time," my dad said.

I avoided eye contact with him as I took my normal seat next to Zion. We made small talk over the course of dinner. Mom said, "Jorge, Sierra's lost a lot of weight so she's going to need some more school uniforms."

"I've seen her in them and she looks fine to me."

I opened up my mouth to protest but from my mom's expression, I closed it. She said, "If she keeps losing at this rate, she's going to be walking around with a big pin in them to keep them up. Do you want our daughter to go around looking tacky?"

My dad dropped his fork on his plate. "Of course not."

"Then please give me the okay to get her some more uniforms."

"Y'all just don't understand how tight the market is right now. Sierra," he turned and said to me, "can you at least wear those for another week? I'll need to make some adjustments and then I'll be glad to get you some new uniforms. Okay?"

I couldn't understand. We were rich so why did my dad act like we couldn't get some uniforms that wouldn't have cost more than two hundred dollars. Something didn't feel right. I needed to find out what was going on. There was something my dad wasn't telling me and from the look on my mom's face, she was left feeling clueless too.

~ 30 ~

The Movement

My mind felt boggled down with not only the situation with my dad, but I felt like I was on information overload due to this reporting period's midterm exams. As we passed each other in the hallway, Cecil asked, "Has Jasmine said anything about me?"

"Hate to burst your bubble, but that would be a no," I responded.

"I didn't figure she did," he said.

"Then why did you ask?" I said, probably sounding more agitated than I should.

"Just curious."

"Well, I need to get to class so I'll chat with you later."

"You sure there will be a later?" he asked.

"Yes, Cecil, now move so I can go," I said, waiting on him to stop blocking the doorway.

When I got to my seat and looked up, Cecil was staring at me from the doorway. He smiled, waved and walked away. I didn't have time to concentrate on Cecil's Jasmine issues. I had a test to pass.

Dance class was a breeze. The routine I choreographed came off flawless. The teacher gave me an "A" on the spot. Britney got a "B" and wasn't too happy about it. "Can you believe it? I decided to do one impromptu move and she took off points for it," Britney said.

"She did say we would have to stick to the moves we outlined for her or else she would take off for them," I said, in the dance instructor's defense.

"But still. The new move was better than what I had originally come up with."

"I agree," I said.

"Look at them. I'm glad now that I made the decision that I did," Britney said, pointing to the opposite side of the gym. Luther stood talking to some girl who, every time you turned around, had her hand grazing his face. Luther didn't attempt to move her hands away. I felt bad that Britney had to witness that.

Britney wiped her teary eyes. "I liked him a lot. I guess after I told him it would be best if we waited, he moved on without me."

I was so not used to being the one comforting Britney but I did my best to do so. "Come on let's go. Remember, don't let him see you sweat." I tried to lighten up the situation.

Britney pulled out her compact mirror, wiped her face and put on some grape lip gloss. "Let's walk the long way," she said.

I had to increase my pace to keep up with Britney. When we got near Luther, Britney said, "Hi Luther and Heather."

Heather spoke, but Luther didn't. I said, "Luther what's wrong? The cat's got your tongue?"

He looked at me and rolled his eyes. I had no idea a boy could roll his eyes like that. He said, "Hi Britney and I forget your friend's name."

"It's Sierra," I said.

"Can I talk to you for a minute?" Britney asked. She looked at Heather and said, "Alone."

Luther turned towards Heather. "It'll only take a minute. I'll catch up with you after school."

Heather said, "You don't owe her an explanation. It is what it is."

I don't know how Britney felt, but I wanted to throw my backpack at her. I laughed to myself at the thought. I could see her falling to the floor head first once my backpack filled with books hit her. That would have been a priceless sight to see. I pretended to fall back so Britney and Luther could have their privacy; although I could hear their entire conversation.

"It looks like I made the right decision," Britney said.

Luther responded, "It's not what it looks like."

I hope Britney didn't fall for it. Even I, Ms. Naive when it comes to relationships, could see through his bull.

Britney brushed her hair away from her face. "I was looking right at you and Heather. You had no problems with her hands in your face. Let me demonstrate." Britney matched Heather's movements from earlier.

Unlike earlier though, Luther pulled away. "You're making a big deal out of nothing."

"You're right. We are nothing. You can forget the possibility of what could have been. Lose my number," Britney said, right before turning to walk away.

He rushed from behind her and blocked her

from walking further. "What am I supposed to do? I'm not going to wait for you forever."

Britney's face had turned red. She began talking with her hands as she spoke. "I almost said 'yes Luther I'll give us a chance', but after witnessing what I saw today I'm so glad I didn't. You're not worth my time."

"Bri wait."

"Move," she snapped.

"Give us a chance. You shot us down before we could get anything started," Luther said.

"Our time is up and will never be again, so for the last time, move out of my way," Britney said.

This time Luther moved. She walked past me. I looked at Luther and sneered. He threw up his middle finger. I continued to smile as I waved at him and then ran to catch up with Britney. Tears were flowing down her face when we got to the bathroom. I wet a paper towel and gave it to her so she could clear her face.

"He's not even worth it," I assured her.

"Sierra, I know. But it doesn't make it easier."

Watching Britney go through her emotions, reminded me of the bleak period I went through with DJ. The life and times of a teenager could be hard, don't let nobody fool you.

~ 31 ~

The Paper

My dad didn't eat dinner with us the rest of the week. We were told he was working. My dad was a hard worker but it was rare he didn't take the time to eat dinner with his family. Now that midterms were over, I had to figure out what was going on with my dad. Since neither he nor my mom was talking, I went to the only source I knew would give me all the information I needed—the Internet.

I was using Britney's computer when the idea popped into my head. I typed in the name Jorge Sanchez. Most of the information talked about the same thing. I was just about to give up hope when a recent article in the Dallas newspaper had a headline—REAL ESTATE MOGUL IN DANGER OF LOSING IT ALL. I clicked on the article, but it was archived. "Bri, can I use your card so I can access this article?"

"Sure," Britney said. Britney placed the fashion magazine she was reading down and retrieved her credit card. "Here you go."

I entered the information required and it didn't take long for the article to download. I printed out a copy just in case the computer went out. Britney was generous to pay for it this time but I wouldn't expect her to do it a second time.

While I read the article online, Britney retrieved the paper off the printer and read the copy. "We're losing everything," I blurted out as I read the article. The article went into details on the affairs of my dad's business.

Britney read out loud, "Sanchez has been a top real estate developer in the Dallas area for over a decade. With the ups and downs in the economy, it seems that this once top developer has been suffering some minor setbacks. According to our sources, what was once thought as minor setbacks, are major. It's not currently clear how much damage this last stock loss affected Sanchez's business holdings, but it's estimated to be in the millions. The outcome will not only affect Sanchez's business but because he outsourced to other small businesses in the area, the fallings out of this spells a major financial disaster for Dallas."

I read out loud the last part of the article. "Sanchez's life is about to change majorly. He's already laid off half of his staff and many more layoffs are foreseen to happen. One of his ex-employees who wants to remain nameless confirmed that the business mogul's reign on top has definitely come to an end. We hope that he has put something aside for a rainy day, because otherwise Sanchez might find himself in the unemployment line."

According to the paper, we were broke. Millions of dollars gone into thin air because of people like Murdoch and other investors who were scheming people. "What's going to happen to us?"

"Sierra, it's going to be okay. It's probably not as bad as the paper makes it out to be. You know how folks can exaggerate things." Britney's attempt to comfort me failed.

My mind thought about the talk my dad had with the family about cutting back. I recalled not being able to buy new uniforms right now. My mom didn't know I knew it, but there was no maid; she was now doing all of the cleaning.

I'm sure most people wouldn't be too concerned

since it seemed as if I lived a pampered life, but if it was the life you had become accustomed to, then it would be easy to see why I felt the way I did. My whole world was turning upside down and there wasn't a thing I could do about it. Right now it seemed the only thing I had in control was my weight. Even with me eating more food than I know I should, the diet pills had me losing weight. I wasn't losing it as fast as I was when I started on them a few weeks ago, but I was still losing.

Britney did her best to comfort me. "Try not to worry. Ask your dad about it when you get home."

"Do you really think he's going to share something with me? I think not." I didn't mean to take out my frustrations on Britney but she was the closest thing to me.

"Maybe my mom knows something. I'll go ask her."

Britney didn't wait for me to respond. She left me alone in her room with my thoughts. I don't know how long I had been sitting there staring at the computer screen. I felt a tap on my shoulder. It made me jump. "Didn't mean to startle you," Ms. Destiny, Britney's mom, said.

"Britney told me about your concerns. I've talked to Maria and she's going to explain everything to you when she comes to pick you up. She should be here shortly."

"Thanks Ms. Destiny."

She hugged me. "You know I love you like you were my own. Try not to worry about anything, okay?"

"That's what Bri keeps telling me."

"Listen to her," she said, winking her eye.

Britney walked back in the room after her mother left. "Thanks Bri," I said.

"That's what friends are for. I hate seeing you like this."

"I didn't come over to talk about my problems. You were supposed to be telling me about Luther remember."

Britney plopped on her bed. "Only because I want you to get your mind off your dad."

I turned around in the chair to face her. "It's not going to work but I'm listening."

Britney said, "Luther has been calling and leaving messages when I don't answer. He's full of crap. I don't see what I ever saw in him in the first place."

I threw my hands up in the air. "He's only the finest boy on the football team. He's not only fine but he's smart. Should I go on?"

Britney placed her face in her hands and then leaned back. "It hurts girl. It hurts."

"Better you find out about him now than later."

Britney looked up at me and said, "Didn't I tell you that once?"

"Once, twice. I lost count," I said, as we laughed.

~ 32 ~

Rumors

My mom picked me up shortly after the conversation I had with Ms. Destiny. I could tell she was nervous because she kept trying to make small talk. I could care less about the weather and at this point, I didn't even want to talk about my favorite subject, fashion.

She turned the music down. "Destiny tells me you girls ran across an article on Jorge."

"Is it true?" I asked, getting straight to the point.

"We will have to ask your dad. I haven't read the article. Destiny gave me a copy of it before I left."

I didn't know if I could believe her or not. She lied to my dad about the amount of money she spent so who's to say she wasn't lying to me about the article.

When we arrived home, my dad and Zion were playing a video game in the den. "Jorge, we need to talk," my mom said in a serious tone.

He said, "Zion, we'll finish this game later or you can play both hands."

"Aww, man, it was just getting good," Zion responded.

I followed them into the living room. My dad mumbled the entire way. I sat on the loveseat, while my parents sat on the couch. My dad said, "What's so important that you had to drag me out the den?" he asked.

Maria reached into her purse and handed him the article. He glanced at the pages. When he looked back up, it looked as if the light in his eyes had disappeared. "I told you to not read the paper," he said to her.

"Mama didn't. I found it on the Internet." It seemed at that moment, my dad finally realized I was still in the room.

"Don't worry yourself about this. I have everything under control. Those are just rumors in that article" he said.

Maria reached over and picked up the papers

out of his lap. She read out loud some of the things in the article. He looked down. "According to this article and the constant lectures I've been getting from you about spending money, I think there's truth somewhere." She threw the paper at him.

He let the paper fall to the floor. "We agreed not to argue in front of the kids remember?"

"A fine time to think of that now. Look at her." She was pointing at me. "Sierra's no longer a little kid. She's old enough to know what's going on."

"Maria, calm down," he said. Even I know not to tell an upset person to calm down because it would only make things worse.

My mom stood up and placed one hand on her hip and the other she used to illustrate her frustrations. "When you sit here and tell me and your daughter the truth is when I will calm down. In the mean time I will say what I want and nobody including you can stop me."

My dad got up and reached for my mom's hand. She stopped pacing the floor. "Sit. I'll tell you what I can."

She sat down and crossed her legs and arms. "We're listening."

My dad looked at me and then back at my mom. "I've had to lay off a lot of the staff because th cost was just too much. We had more money going out than we had coming in so I had to cut back somewhere."

"Jorge some of those people have been working for you since day one."

He hung his head low. "How do you think it made me feel? I prided myself on being what I called a family organization and then I had to fire some of my family."

"Why didn't you tell me?" she asked.

"My business is separate from our relationship."

Her hands flew up in the air. "Not when I have to listen to you complain about me spending money. I've been spending money like this for years and you had no problems with it."

"You're right, because the money was flowing in. Now we all, including you, must make adjustments."

"If you would have only told me this, then I wouldn't have gone behind your back and did all that shopping," she admitted.

"You should have trusted me and not did it period when I asked you to cut back."

Once again I was invisible as I sat there and listened to them go back and forth. I had enough so I yelled to get their attention. My dad said, "Young lady, you have lost your mind if you think you're going to raise your voice at me."

"Jorge, stop talking to her like that. Can't you see all of this is stressing her out? She's lost weight because of all of this." My mom could be melodramatic. I lost weight not because of my dad but because those diet pills really worked.

Zion walked in the room. "What's wrong?"

Maria motioned for him to come to her. She wrapped her arms around him. "Nothing baby. We're just having a family discussion and we got a little loud."

"Zion, go back in the den. I'll be there shortly and I'll play another game with you," my dad said.

Once it was clear Zion was no longer in ear shot, my dad said, "I was hoping I would be able to put this off."

My heart pounded fast as I waited to see what news he had to share. Maria tapped her fingers on the side of the couch. We sat. We waited and heard nothing as silence fell over the room. After a few minutes of silence, my dad said, "We might have to move."

"Noooo," I said, as tears formed in my eyes.

My mom said, "Jorge, I thought we were okay. Not our home. Can't you sell something . . . anything? But our home Jorge?"

My dad originally said they were just rumors, but if we have to move, the words in the paper were true. I felt betrayed.

~ 33 ~

Calm After the Storm

I walked back to my room in a zombie state of mind. I was just going through the motions. I think I zoned out when he said we would have to move. I had been in this house since I was four years old. I couldn't imagine living anywhere else. The only regret about this house was the fact my real mom didn't get a chance to experience the beauty of it. I'm not an outdoors person but I do enjoy walking outside and admiring the beauty of the flowers. During certain times of the year, there would be apples on the tree my dad had planted in the back when Zion was born.

The house held so many memories and most of them were of my childhood. At fifteen years old, I could not see myself living anywhere else right now. How would I tell my two best friends that we were no longer rich? Would I still be able to go to Plano High? I had so many questions for my dad, but didn't want to go back into the den. I left both parents arguing. Neither one was willing to back down.

I stayed in my room off and on for the majority of the weekend. I was too depressed to talk to Britney or Jasmine. They sent me text messages and I returned a few, but even my phone and the Internet didn't give me any peace. I slept as much as I could because that's the only time I didn't think about my problems or feel the pounding in my head caused by the diet pills.

The alarm went off way too soon for me. It was Monday and as much as I dreaded going to school because I hadn't slept well, it would be a welcome reprieve. My mom barely said two words to me before dropping me off at school. The most she said was "hi" and "good-bye." I could tell she had been crying because her eyes were bloodshot red.

Britney and Jasmine were waiting in our usual spot as soon as I walked on the school campus. I took a seat by Jasmine. "You look like you lost your best friend," Jasmine commented.

I saw Britney kick her. Jasmine said, "I'm just

saying. We're girls so we should be able to tell each other the truth."

Jasmine wasn't aware of the article about my dad. I had sworn Britney to secrecy and since Jasmine was asking questions, it looked as if Britney respected my wishes. I said, "It's my dad."

Jasmine said, "You're having dad trouble too. This new woman my dad is seeing wants to meet me. I don't want to meet any of 'his' women."

"Duh. It's not about you now. It's about our Sierra," Britney said.

I told Jasmine what we read. I left out the part about me having to move. I had not come to grips with that fact yet and somehow talking about it would make it more real, so I opted not to.

"Wow, I had no idea," Jasmine said.

Britney said, "If you need anything, we got your back."

"Yes. Lunch money. Whatever. We got you," Jasmine said.

I stood up. "I'm not a charity case yet."

"We didn't mean anything by it," Jasmine said.

"I'll catch up with y'all later," I responded. I couldn't face my friends. I felt ashamed of the situation my family found itself in.

The homeroom class was empty when I arrived.

I sat at my desk and replayed the things my dad said Saturday. "Boo," Cameron said. He laughed because I jumped.

He continued on to say. "Is there anything you want to talk about?"

"Not to you," I mumbled.

"I didn't hear you," Cameron said.

"Nothing. I'm cool."

"Can I call you sometime?" he asked.

I really wasn't in the mood to deal with Cameron but I said, "Sure." At that point I would have said anything to get him out of my face. His sidekick slash girlfriend walked in with her nose turned up.

Lauren planted a kiss on Cameron's lips. I hoped Ms. Hogan would walk in the room. They both would be in trouble, but that's what Cameron would get for being with her instead of me. I shifted my body in the seat. I pulled out my cell phone. I had several text messages from Cecil. He sent a few jokes. I couldn't help but chuckle as I read some of them. I sent him a quick message. His messages came at the right time. It's as if he knew I needed cheering up even though he and I hadn't talked much lately. I didn't want to hear him go on and on about a lost cause, his mission to be with Jasmine.

I waited for Britney and Jasmine outside the

class door after homeroom. We had a pop quiz and I had finished mine prior to them. I observed some of the other students in the hallway as I waited. I wondered what their background was. Were they poor, middle class, rich? If they were poor; how did they deal with not getting everything they wanted? My dad made sure I did chores and other things but I didn't know how to go without stuff. It would be hard to adjust to. I thought this situation was just temporary. I thought soon I could go back to ordering things off the Internet and shopping at the Galleria with my girls.

"I think I aced it," I heard Britney say, as she and Jasmine walked out of the classroom.

"Me too," Jasmine responded.

"I have so much on my mind. I would be happy with a C right now," I said.

Britney said, "My mom always says that there's calm after the storm."

"But when will this storm ever end?" I asked out loud.

No one had the answer. We all walked away to our next class in silence. The only noise heard was the kids chattering in the hallways.

~ 34 ~

Kiss Me through the Phone

Later Monday night I couldn't sleep. I didn't feel like talking to Jasmine or Britney so I dialed Cecil's number. His ringback tone had been changed to the once popular song by Soulja Boy. I sang along with it until I heard Cecil's voice. "I didn't think you would ever call," he said.

"This is Sierra not Jasmine," I assured him.

"I know who it is."

"Oh. Well what's up?" I asked.

"Just finished doing some homework. What's up with you?" Cecil asked.

"Bored."

"Oh I get it. Your friends weren't available so you called me," he teased.

"No, it's not even like that," I said. "We haven't really talked in awhile so I was just calling to see what was going on with you. To find out if you had finally given up on Jasmine."

"To answer your question, yes. I realized, maybe a little late, that going after Jasmine was as you put it 'a lost cause.'"

"It's about time. We should celebrate," I said, teasing him.

"I'll hold you to it."

"Well it's late and I'm really not supposed to be on the phone," I said. I was not sure why I felt a little tingle in my spine when he told me he was no longer feeling Jasmine like that anymore.

"Sierra, you made my night by calling. I hope you know how special you are."

"If I didn't know any better Cecil I would say you were flirting," I responded.

"And you would be correct. Good night," he said right before hanging up the phone.

I stared at my cell phone for a few minutes. Once I laid my head on my pillows it didn't take long for me to go to sleep. My dad was gone by the time I made it downstairs for breakfast. Zion whined, "Why can't I go on the field trip?"

My mom said, "Because we will be going on a family trip there and it doesn't make sense to pay for you to go to San Antonio twice, now does it?"

I'm sure she was lying because from what my dad said, it would be a long time before we took any more family vacations. It makes it seem like the fat camp retreats she took me on this past summer were well worth the trips.

I was about to take a bite out of my biscuit when I realized that I hadn't taken my diet pills. I quickly put the biscuit down. I fumbled in my backpack for the pills I had wrapped up in a tissue. I had the pills in my hand to take when Maria said, "What are those?"

"Nothing," I lied. I put them in my mouth to take.

"Spit them out," she said.

I did as I was told. It was disgusting to see my saliva mixed with the white pills. "Young lady, I'm going to ask you one more time. What are these?"

Since I had been busted, there was no reason to lie. I said, "Just some diet pills."

"Sierra Ann Sanchez. Do you know how dangerous these pills can be?"

"They haven't done anything to me," I said. I didn't tell her about the dizziness or the slight headaches. I was sure that was because I was losing so much weight. I was now thirty pounds lighter than I was prior to school starting.

She stood in front of me. "Look at you. You're losing weight so fast, if I didn't know better, I would think you were a crackhead. Shoot, taking these diet pills is just as dangerous as crack."

"But . . ." I said.

"But nothing. Go to your room now and hand me the bottle."

Zion was in the next room so I hoped he hadn't heard our exchange. If so, he would definitely tell my dad. When I ordered the pills, I would order two bottles at a time. I retrieved one of the used bottles from under my bed and left the full bottle in the hidden location. There was no reason for me to give her both bottles.

She stood at the bottom of the stairway with her hand held out. I placed the bottle in her hands. "Do you know this could have killed you and we wouldn't have had a clue what happened to you?"

I listened to her go on and on about the dangers of taking diet pills. "I'm not going to tell your dad about this, but don't let me ever hear of you doing something so dangerous again."

"Yes ma'am."

"Now get your stuff so I can drop you off at school."

I retrieved my backpack from near the dining room table. I got lectured again on the way to school. She added, "I know I've been on you about your weight, but dear, you're losing too much weight too fast. Granted, you can never be too thin, but doing it by using pills, it can cause you health problems that you may not be able to get rid of."

I could hear her talking, but I was happy with the fast results and I had no intention of stopping. I got to eat what I wanted and still lost weight in the process, so why should I stop taking them? What my mom said went in one ear and then out the other. I was so glad to see the school campus. "You can let me out here. I need the exercise anyway," I said.

Exercise was the key word. She let me out near the curb. I waved bye and rushed up the walkway to the school yard. I must have been early because Britney and Jasmine weren't there yet. "There goes the most beautiful girl at Plano High," I heard Cecil say as he walked near me. I looked around to see who he was talking about.

"I was talking about you," he said, as if he read my mind.

He must want something. "Tell me what kind of favor you need. You don't have to give me compliments to get them."

"A date."

Cecil threw me off guard with his request. *A date. Wow. I wasn't expecting that.*

~ 35 ~

What's Love Got to Do with It?

Before I could give Cecil a response, Jasmine and Britney showed up. He greeted them and then left.

Jasmine said, "I didn't mean to interrupt."

"There wasn't anything going on to interrupt," I said.

"Didn't look like it to me," Britney said.

"Looks can be deceiving," I responded.

The first bell rang. I lagged behind Jasmine and Britney as Cecil and I were the main topic of their conversation. They were speculating but at this point there was nothing to speculate about. Number one, I was not interested in Cecil. I was interested in Cameron. Cameron's not calling me even after I gave him the okay to do so bothered me a little, but not as much as it would have a few months ago.

After first period, I needed to take a bathroom detour. I found Marcus' girlfriend crying and mending a bruise on her arm. It looked like she was having a difficult time doing it, so I offered to help. "What happened?" I asked, while opening the bandage for her.

"I fell," Cassie said in a low voice.

I didn't believe that and neither did she. "I'm good at keeping secrets," I said.

She looked at the door. When it didn't look like anyone was going to come in she said, "Marcus did this to me, but please don't tell anybody."

"He did what?"

"I knew I shouldn't have told you. Nobody believes me," Cassie said, slightly above a whisper.

I didn't know what to do. "I do believe you. It's just that . . . Why? How long has this been going on?" I asked.

"Too long."

"Let's go to the office. Maybe they can do something about him."

"No," she said, as she grabbed my arm with a tight grip.

"We have to do something."

Cassie seemed to be gathering her strength from a place I was unfamiliar with. "This is my problem. I'll handle it."

She said it so forcefully; it made me move back a little. "If you need my help, I'm here. Britney's here for you too," I added.

"She's the problem," she said.

I shook my head a few times. "Back up. What do you mean by that?" I asked.

"Your friend Britney is the reason why Marcus beats me. He wants her more than he wants me and he tells me that each time he hits me."

I was blown away with the news. "I will tell Britney and maybe she can help."

"It'll only make things worse. Remember the day I saw you both in the gym. Well, Marcus thought I had said something to you all and he almost broke my arm that night."

I removed my notebook, tore a sheet a paper out of it, and wrote my number down. I handed it to

Cassie. "Take this. This is my number. If he starts hitting you again, call me. He can't take both of us down."

She placed my number in her back pack. A hall monitor walked into the bathroom and said, "Ladies, the bell rang for your class five minutes ago."

On the way to class, I pulled out my cell phone and sent a quick text message to Britney so she would do her best to meet me for lunch without taking her time. By lunch time, I was ready to burst with the information I had learned.

Jasmine tried to dominate the entire conversation during lunch so I said, "I hate to stop the Jasmine Drama Show but there's something real important I need to talk about."

Jasmine rolled her eyes. I rolled mine right back. I said, "I saw Cassie in the bathroom this morning and she didn't look too good."

Jasmine said, "Who's Cassie?"

Britney responded, "Marcus' girlfriend. Remember we told you about her?"

"Oh, yeah."

I said, "Well she had bruises on her arms caused by him."

"I knew it. I knew he was abusing her," Britney blurted.

"What he needs is a good old butt whooping. We can take him," Jasmine said. Jasmine seemed to always be ready for a fight.

I repeated to them what Cassie had shared with me earlier. They were shocked. Britney said, "Wait until I confront him."

I said, "Do you really think it's safe? He's beating her so I'm sure he has no problems hitting you."

Jasmine said, "He preys on the weak. Something must be weak about this Cassie."

Britney said, "I discussed this with my mom and abuse has happened to the strongest woman."

"Let me know when you want to confront him. He can't take all of us down," Jasmine said.

"I agree. We'll all confront him."

"I say let's do it after school," Jasmine said.

Britney responded, "It sounds like a plan, unless I see him beforehand."

"Let's hope you don't. We might have to protect him from you instead of the other way around," I said,

"And he once called himself my boyfriend."

Jasmine commented, "I just saw the movie

What's Love Got to Do with It. What Cassie needs to do is go upside Marcus' head one good time and he'll stop."

"She needs to leave Marcus alone period. Forget being a ride or die chick," I added.

~ 36 ~

Operation Marcus

I saw Marcus in passing between classes. It took all I had not to go push him or hit him with a stick or something. He was a boy. He had no business putting his hands on a girl. I rushed outside as soon as I got out of my last class. Jasmine and Britney showed up a few minutes later. "Where is he?" Jasmine asked.

"Calm down. Save that energy for when we do see him," Britney said.

"Here he comes," I said, as I noticed him walking down the hall.

"Move to the side so we can make sure he's out the doors before we confront him," Britney said.

We walked off the steps and waited for him to

reach the bottom steps. Britney walked up to him and said, "Marcus let me talk to you for a minute."

"What's up Bri? Ladies?" he said, oblivious to the berating he was about to get.

Britney started pressing her fingers into his chest. "You want to beat on a girl. Hit me. Let me show you how it will feel when someone fights back."

"I don't know what you're talking about. Bri, you need to chill with that finger of yours," he said.

His facial expression changed so I could tell he was getting upset. Jasmine and I walked up as a reminder to him that Britney was not there alone. "Hit me," I said.

Jasmine said, "No, hit me if you're bad."

Marcus said, "You girls are crazy, all of you. I don't know what is going on but y'all need to step back or suffer the consequences."

"Was that a threat?" I asked.

Jasmine replayed the video on her cell phone. "I think it was."

Marcus reached for it. "Give that to me."

Jasmine stepped back several steps. "I don't think so."

"I was not threatening you."

"Well it doesn't sound like it from the video,"

Britney said, as she now stood with her arms folded.

"I remember a certain cousin of yours posting a video online. I wonder how many hits I'll get if I posted this online," Jasmine said. She was referring to Marcus' cousin DJ. He had posted a video trying to make both me and Jasmine look bad.

"This is ridiculous. First y'all accuse me of abusing Cassie and then this," Marcus said.

Britney said, "We never said you abused her. But when you're guilty, you're bound to tell the truth eventually."

Marcus had said too much. He knew he was guilty. He rushed past us and got on the bus.

"I hope we scared him enough so that he won't hit Cassie again," I said.

"Me too," Jasmine said.

"Thanks. You all did what I didn't have the courage to do," Cassie said, as she walked up behind us.

"We got your back," Britney said. "I'm sorry Marcus still has unresolved feelings for me and is taking it out on you. It's not fair. No girl deserves to be beat."

"Well, he's going to be real upset with me now."

Jasmine said, "Stop taking his calls. Don't let him come over. Avoid him."

"Easier said than done. I love him. He seems to know what buttons to push to make me forgive him."

I said, "Do you like getting beat up?"

She shook her head back and forth and said, "No. Of course not."

"Then there you go. Love doesn't hurt. Not like that," I said.

Britney said, "The three of us are like sisters. We protect each other even if it means making the other person upset. We want you to know that if you vow to leave Marcus, we will have your back."

Britney looked at me and Jasmine. We agreed. Britney said, "So what are you going to do?"

"If you promise to have my back, talk to me when I get the urge to call him, I'll do it."

"We got it."

We all exchanged numbers. Later that night, Britney called both me and Jasmine on the three-way. "Marcus has left me threatening messages all night. I guess Cassie broke it off with him and now he feels like it's my fault."

"Dude is thrown off," Jasmine said.

"Crazy with a capitol C," I added.

Britney said, "I told him off several times but then I got tired of answering my phone. He keeps messing with me; I'll call the police and tell them he's harassing me."

Jasmine said, "I have a detective's number if you need it."

"I hope it doesn't come to that," Britney responded.

I couldn't understand why Britney didn't report Marcus' behavior. She seemed to still have a soft spot for him.

"The twins are calling me," Britney said. She ended the call to go see about her little brother and sister.

Cassie called me. "Thanks for having my back. Marcus wasn't thrilled when I told him I didn't want to see him anymore."

"He'll be alright," I responded.

"I was glad I did it over the phone, because he was cursing and screaming. There's no telling what he would have done to me if I had been sitting right there."

"It's done, that's all that matters," I said.

It looked like operation get Cassie to leave Marcus alone was a success, but at what cost?

~ 37 ~

Call Block

I tossed and turned all night. When I did fall asleep, I had nightmare after nightmare with Marcus' face being at the center of each one. The Marcus situation, made me forget my issues at home. I was like a zombie as my mom drove me to school the next morning. My mom's attempt to get me to open up was unsuccessful. I wasn't in the best of moods. I gave her a weak wave after getting out of the car.

"You're a hard person to catch up with," Cecil said, as he rushed up to me on the sidewalk.

"You must have dialed the wrong number because my phone hasn't rung."

"Check your messages," he said.

"Cecil, so I won't be rude, I'm really not in a good mood right now. I don't want to take it out on you."

"I can handle it," he said.

"But it's not fair to you."

"Let me decide what's fair and what's not."

"I never want to treat you like Jasmine did."

Cecil grabbed my hand. I turned around to face him. "I know in my heart you would never do me like that."

My heart fluttered. I temporarily forgot about my bad night and the things going on with my family, and Marcus. Cameron walked by. "I knew you were lying about seeing each other," he said.

I held Cecil's hand. "We don't have to run anything past you."

"I know," he stuttered. "I thought you . . . I . . . well it doesn't matter now does it?" he asked.

"No, it doesn't," I said. What was I thinking? Cecil and I had nothing going on, but the fact that Cameron thought I was waiting on him irked me, so I had no choice but to use Cecil.

Once Cameron was out of our earshot, I turned to Cecil and said, "I'm sorry. He made me so mad. I didn't mean to use you like that."

"If it'll get you to hold my hand, use me baby use me."

I laughed. "You're so silly."

"Only for you," he responded.

Marcus walked by giving me an evil look. Cecil noticed. "What's up with that?"

"He's probably mad because his girlfriend broke up with him." I shared with Cecil what had transpired.

"Oh, he better not try to lay a hand on you or he'll have me to deal with," Cecil said. The way he said it, I knew he meant it, although it was hard to picture Cecil fighting anyone.

"Thanks. It's good to know somebody has my back."

The first bell rang so Cecil walked me to class. Britney and Jasmine both showed up after the tardy bell. Ms. Hogan didn't seem too happy about it. She gave them extra work to show her disapproval. I felt bad for them, but it was better them than me. I had enough homework to do.

During lunch, Britney shared with us that she had to call the cell phone company about blocking Marcus' number. He had left over twenty messages in her voice mail. "He's crazy," I said.

"Speaking of crazy, there he is," Jasmine said, looking near the doorway.

Marcus saw us looking at him. He punched one of his fists into his hand and then pointed in our direction. Jasmine held up her cell phone as a reminder to him of the video recording she had of him threatening us. He moved away from the door.

"I don't know who he thinks he's scaring," Britney said.

I told them about my slight run in with him earlier. They both were shocked at Cecil's comments. Jasmine said, "I told you he liked you."

"I don't want to be his rebound love."

"Girl, what Cecil had for me was infatuation, not love."

I agreed with her. I had never thought of Cecil in a boyfriend sort of way. I lied. I had a little bit, but there was no sense in having my thoughts roam too far in that direction. At the time he seemed to be all about Jasmine.

Jasmine had a point. She didn't like him and he said he no longer liked her in that manner. Maybe I should start flirting back, to see where it lead. I thought my sophomore year would be drama-free but boy was I wrong.

Cecil waited for me after school. Jasmine and

Britney encouraged me to talk to him. "See y'all later," I said, as I allowed him to walk me to the car. I knew my mom would have questions but Cecil was a good guy so she shouldn't have a problem with him.

"Don't make me have to call block you now," I teased, as he promised to call me later.

"If I ever become a pest, let me know and I'll stop calling you," he said.

Talking to Cecil was refreshing. I didn't feel stressed out. I didn't wonder if he liked me. I didn't worry if I was small enough. I didn't have to wonder if he wanted to be with me now that I had lost all of the weight.

"Mom, I want you to meet Cecil."

"Hi Cecil," she said.

Cecil responded, "Hi Mrs. Sanchez. I walked over because I wanted to meet Sierra's mom."

"Oh, how sweet. Nice meeting you, Cecil."

Cecil whispered, "Guess, I'll see you later."

"He seems like a nice kid," my mom said, once I was in the car.

"He's alright."

"Oh he must be too nice for you. I used to love the bad boys too. But bad boys bring nothing but trouble. I was in my twenties before I realized that.

Fortunately by the time I met your father, I had my priorities straight."

"Speaking of my dad, are we moving or not?" I asked.

"I wish I knew. He hasn't said anything else. Whenever I bring it up, he responds 'I'm handling my business so let me.' I swear your dad can be a handful at times."

They were a match made in heaven because so was she.

~ 38 ~

Time for a Change

"Sierra you're losing absolutely too much weight," my mom said. "I'm really concerned about you."

"I'm fine."

"Did you order any more of those pills?" she asked.

"No," I said. Well, I wasn't lying. I still had some pills left over from my last order. She had no clue about it and I had no intentions of telling her.

"I've taken all of your uniforms and gotten them altered. Your dad refused to buy new ones."

"That's going to look so tacky," I said. I couldn't believe it. I'm used to being on the cutting edge of fashion. Things were bad when I couldn't get a new uniform.

"I'm afraid there's some more news. Your Dancing Diamond fees aren't going to be paid next semester unless business turns around."

"Well I might as well be dead right now. I won't be able to show my face. The fees are only two hundred dollars."

"Your father has made it clear that we have to cut back in all areas. In fact, no more beauty salon trips. From now on, I will be doing your hair and mine."

At the mention of hair, my hand automatically flew up to my hair. I just got it relaxed. I wasn't sure I wanted my mom relaxing my hair. I envisioned seeing all of my hair fall on the floor. I twinged at the thought. This had to be the twilight zone.

"What about my allowance? Will I still be getting an allowance?" I asked.

"Your dad loves making me look like the bad guy. Sorry dear, but there will be no more allowances."

Life as I knew it had truly come to an end. My mom went on to say, "I'm to get all of your credit cards so there will be no temptation to use them."

I reached in my wallet and removed the cards. I didn't touch the emergency card. She said, "He wants that back too."

I reluctantly removed it. I handed it to her. She placed them in her purse sitting next to her. I was blinking back the tears. I turned my head to look out the window. I didn't want her to see me cry.

She said, "I feel the same way you do. I got all of my cards taken away except for one and that's so I can buy stuff for the house when needed."

"What are we going to do?" I asked.

She patted me on top of the hand. "We're going to pull ourselves together and make whatever adjustments we need. I'm going to do whatever I can to hold on to our home."

Before I realized it, the tears that I had been able to hold back flooded my face. "But why now? Everything was perfect."

"It's not our job to question why. God would say, 'Why not you?' Everything happens for a reason. God never puts anything on you that you aren't able to bear."

That might be true, but I sure didn't feel like it. My world was turning upside down and it didn't seem like I could do a thing about it. Times like this I missed my birth mother. I could still smell the sweet scent of her hair when she held me in her arms.

When we arrived home, I went straight to my room. I turned out the light and got in the bed. I didn't wake up until Zion shook me. "Mom says hurry up. Dinner's going to be cold waiting on you," Zion said.

"I'm not feeling well. I'll eat later," I said, as I pulled the cover over my head.

Zion left but returned a few minutes later. "Mom says you better get your butt down there and now."

"No, she didn't," I said.

Zion thought it was funny. "No, she didn't. I just wanted to see if you were faking. She said that's cool. Let her know if you need something."

"Is Dad down there?" I asked.

"Nope. He called and won't be back until real late."

"Okay, well enjoy dinner."

Zion was almost out the door when he paused and turned around. "Are we moving?"

"Why? What did you hear?" I said, as I removed the cover from over my head.

"I heard mom talking to someone on the phone about it. She was real upset."

"Just be prepared for whatever," I responded.

Zion left. I was left alone with my thoughts.

I had dozed off. When I woke up, my dad was sitting in a chair watching me. "Sierra, I'm so sorry. Maria told me you weren't feeling well. I feel like it's all my fault."

The look on his face saddened me. "Dad, it's not your fault." Although I couldn't understand how he got in this situation, I knew in my heart it wasn't his fault. His cell phone rang.

He told the caller on the other end, "I'm selling a lot of things. Some property is hard to get rid of. I'm taking a loss, but I would rather do that than lose everything."

I wondered if our home was one of the things he was selling. When his call ended, I asked him.

He responded, "Right now, the house is not going to be touched, but with things the way they are, I can't make any promises. Just be prepared."

It was easier for him to say. How does one prepare herself for a life without all the luxuries she had become accustomed to? How does one prepare herself for possibly losing her friends because they no longer were on the same social level? How does one prepare herself to go from living in a mansion to the ghetto? *I can't. I won't. I need a miracle.*

~ 39 ~

The Chocolate Factory

"Jasmine, I might need to get that detective's number from you because lately everywhere I turn I see Marcus right there," Britney said the next day at lunch. I followed the direction of her eyes. There sat Marcus and his friends. He seemed to be paying close attention to our table.

"I haven't seen Cassie since she broke up with him," I said.

"I'm going to call her," Jasmine said. "What's her number?"

"She's probably in school now," I said.

"Duh. I'm talking about later."

I retrieved the number from my phone and gave it to Jasmine. "Call us on the three-way when you find out something," I said.

"Now that's a nice piece of chocolate right there," Britney said.

I turned around to see who she was looking at. My mouth dropped open. I loved it when Cecil didn't wear his glasses. During the course of the school year, he would flip back and forth between contacts and glasses. He didn't have the backpack he normally had and I could see the waves in his closely cropped hair. When he walked, he appeared as if he was gliding. He had some swagger. Swagger I hadn't seen before.

Jasmine said, "Watch out now. Girl, he's headed straight for you."

I turned around and wiped the drool from my mouth. I pretended to be in a deep conversation with my friends. "What's up ladies?" he asked. "Do you mind if I sit in that vacant chair?"

Jasmine said, "I don't have a problem with it, if they don't."

Britney said, "Its fine with me. What about you Sierra?"

I looked up. "Oh, sure. No problem. Have a seat."

Britney said, "Well I have some notes I need to

go over for my next class so I'm going to bounce early."

Jasmine said, "Me too. See you two later."

Just like that, my two best friends had abandoned me. I was now sitting alone with Cecil. I asked, "So what's with the new do? Who are you trying to impress?" I wanted to touch the top of his head and rub his waves.

"She's sitting right next to me."

"Is she now?" I asked, twirling around the straw in my hand. I was embarrassed when it hit the floor.

Cecil picked it up and placed it on his tray. He handed me his straw. Our hands touched and I couldn't keep my eyes off him. I needed a distraction so I placed the straw in my drink and looked away as I finished it.

"I think that's all that's in there. I can get you another one if you like," he said.

"No, I'm cool. I need to lay off the sodas anyway," I responded.

"Me too. See, another thing we have in common."

Lauren stopped by our table. "Isn't this cute? The two lovebirds."

"Yes, we are definitely cute," I said, as I looked at Cecil and winked my eye.

That shut Lauren up. She moved quickly away from our table. I laughed and so did Cecil. "Remind me to stay on your good side," Cecil teased.

Cameron stopped by our table. "Do you two mind if I sit with y'all?" he asked.

Before responding I asked, "Your girlfriend's over there. Why don't you sit with her?"

He stuttered, "Well . . . see . . . we are no longer seeing each other."

"Man, have a seat," Cecil said.

I looked at him like he had lost his mind. If Cecil was trying to win points with me, having Cameron at our table wasn't going to get him any. Besides, if anything, Cameron was his competition. He shouldn't want Cameron anywhere near me.

"So are you two together or just friends?" Cameron asked once he got situated.

Cecil responded, "We're friends who are exploring the possibilities."

"Oh I see," Cameron responded. "Sierra, you're awfully quiet."

"I don't have much to say," I responded.

"Fellows, you two can keep each other company. I need to go to the restroom before my next class."

"I'll get your tray," Cecil volunteered.

"No, I'll get it," Cameron said.

"I'll save you both the trouble. I'll get rid of my own tray."

I left them both at the table and made a direct beeline to the bathroom as soon as I emptied my tray. I reapplied some lip gloss and headed to my next class.

It was ironic that now that I was feeling Cecil, Cameron wanted to drop Lauren and try to pursue me. I don't like playing second to anyone. I did that enough with DJ. Cameron would have to do a lot to make me consider being with him now. I realized now that I really didn't know much about Cameron. There's more to a guy than his looks. *Wow, boy have I grown.* The guy should have other stuff going on.

I mentally compared Cameron against Cecil. Number one, Cameron wasn't as smart as Cecil. His personality was okay, but his corny jokes could grate on your nerves. During the mental comparison, Cecil had it going on. Cameron, not so much.

Either way it went, both of the guys were like chocolate—delightful in their own way.

~ 40 ~

Decisions, Decisions

"So who do you want?" Jasmine asked me later that night on the three-way.

"It's not like I have to make a decision right now. I just thought it was interesting that both were trying to impress me today. Cecil wrote me a poem but I can't get to it because it's on my phone. I'll forward it to you," I said.

Britney said, "This is what you wanted. You've lost the weight and now you got guys vying for your attention."

Britney sounded like she had a little animosity. I expected it from Jasmine, but not her. Maybe I was tired and when you're tired, every single thing had the possibility of getting on your nerves.

My cell phone rang. It was Cameron. I let his call go to voice mail. A few minutes later, it was Cecil. "I'll talk to y'all later."

"Who is that?" Jasmine asked.

"Cecil."

"Later," Britney said and quickly disconnected my call.

"What's up?" I asked when I clicked back over to talk to Cecil.

Cecil responded, "I have a question. Would you consider being my girlfriend?"

I didn't respond. I didn't know how to respond. I liked Cecil. In fact, I was beginning to like him a lot, but girlfriend, I wasn't too sure about that. It may be too soon. "Sierra are you there?" he asked when I didn't respond.

"Cecil, let me get back with you."

"Okay. I'm willing to wait. At least you didn't immediately say no, so that means I have a chance."

My phone rang again. It was Cameron. "Cecil, I got to go. We'll talk tomorrow."

"Good night," I said, right before clicking over. "Hello."

Cameron responded, "If you didn't answer this time, I was going to assume you were avoiding me."

"Who me?" I laughed.

"Sorry, it took me so long to come to my senses."

"I didn't know you were interested," I said.

"I've been interested since the first day of school," Cameron confessed.

"If so, why did you hook up with Lauren?" I wasn't buying the crap coming out of his mouth.

"She was giving up the goodies and you, well, you're a good girl."

"Then why are you so interested in me now if you know I'm not giving it up?" I asked.

"Because there's just something about you. Do you know how beautiful you are? Guys are always talking about you. Most guys are afraid to approach you."

Really? "Well thanks for the compliment, but I want a guy to want to be with me for more than my looks," I responded.

Cameron said, "Just give me a chance. You and I would be good together."

"Well I don't know you. We're in the same homeroom class. I see you in passing. That's about all I know about you," I admitted.

He got quiet on the phone for a few seconds. He then said, "I have two brothers and two sisters. I'm in the middle. My middle name is Clay. I love everything Michael Jackson. I wish I could have seen him in concert before he died."

"I love Michael Jackson too. My parents made sure I listened to his music and watched his videos," I said. I recalled the day that he died. There were mourners all around the world. I had never seen anything like it. The newscast announcement that the king of pop was dead left a deep void in music.

We chatted about other music artists we liked. We had those in common.

"Sierra, what did I tell you about that phone?" my dad said when he walked into my room, catching me off guard.

"Got to go," I said, without waiting on Cameron to respond.

"Hi Dad. I didn't know you were home," I said.

"I just got here and saw the light from under your door. Tomorrow might be Friday, but you still have school, so go to bed."

"Yes, sir." I saluted him.

"Come on now. All of that's not necessary. Good night sweetie," he said.

"Good night, Dad."

He waited for me to put my cell phone on the table next to my bed before turning off the light and leaving. I got under the covers and dreamed that there was a fight between Cameron and Cecil over me. The alarm beeped waking me out of my sleep before I could find out who won.

The next morning, Cecil and Cameron made it a point to locate me before school started. Britney and Jasmine seemed to be annoyed at the attention I was getting. I had been so wrapped up in my world; I forgot to ask Jasmine about Cassie. "Fellows, I'll catch up with y'all later. I need to talk to my girls."

Jasmine pretended to be appalled. "Bri, can you believe she has time for us?"

Britney said, "I know. I'm just as shocked as you are."

"Y'all need to quit. Jas, what did Cassie say when you called her?"

"She finally called me back last night. She told her mom what had been happening so her mom switched her to another school."

"Wow. That's a shame that she got run off like that," I said.

"She said Marcus had threatened to choke her if he saw her."

I didn't know what to say. Cassie had made the right decision leaving Plano High. I don't know what I would have done if I had been faced with the same situation.

~ 41 ~

He's Bad

It's Friday and I was glad for the school day to end. I got a little depressed when I thought about the fact that I would no longer be having sleepovers at my house. In fact, I didn't know how much longer I would have a house to go to. Cecil walked me to the bus. "I'll be at the game. If you want to sit together, just send me a text message."

"I will," I responded. I went up the stairs of the bus. I took my seat and looked out the window. Cecil waved at me. Jasmine and Britney walked on. Jasmine took a seat next to me. "Your boy is wide open for you."

"I guess," I responded. "He'll be at the game."

"So what are you going to do?" Britney asked. Jasmine didn't know about Cecil's question.

"I haven't decided," I responded.

"Why am I the only one in the dark? What are you talking about?" Jasmine asked.

Since more and more kids were now on the bus, I had to whisper. "Cecil and Cameron both asked me to be their girlfriend. Well Cecil outright did and Cameron hinted around about it."

"Cameron is a bad boy, so if I were you, I would pick Cecil," Jasmine said.

"But you're not me," I snapped.

"Ouch," she said. She moved back as if I slapped her.

"Sorry. I didn't mean to snap."

"Welcome to the club. It's hard choosing when you have so many choices," Jasmine said. She took out her compact mirror to check her makeup and hair.

"I like them both, but in different ways."

"Listen to Jas. Bad boys are not healthy for you. They will break your heart every time," Britney said, as she looked at Luther flirt with one of the cheerleaders.

After we danced in front of the crowd, I sent Cecil a text message. He was already sitting in the area where our team members were scheduled to be seated. I don't know how he got a seat in our area, but was glad. I scanned the crowd. He saw me first because I saw him wave. "Bri, there he is. Come on."

We climbed the steps and made our way to where he was seated. "Thanks for saving two seats," I said.

"I figured you and Britney would be together," he said.

"That was real thoughtful of you," Britney said. She gave me the thumbs up sign without Cecil seeing her.

I took my seat next to Cecil. "What would you ladies like to drink or eat?" he asked.

"Nothing," I responded.

"Come on. You were out there dancing your butt off. I know you should be thirsty."

"Since you twisted my arm, bring me a strawberry drink and some nachos," I responded.

Britney said, "I'll have the same."

I said, "You're not going to be able to carry all of that, so I'll go with you." I looked at Britney. "We'll be back. Don't let anybody take our seats."

After saying "excuse me" countless number of times, we finally made our way to the concession stand. "I could have figured out how to carry all of this myself," Cecil said.

"Maybe I wanted to be alone with you," I said.

"Did you?" he asked.

"I've made a decision, but promise me no matter what the decision is we will always be friends."

Cecil paused and then responded, "Promise."

Just like the soap operas, I left him hanging. "I'll wait until after the game to give you my answer. That way we can all have a good time."

On the way back to the stands with our food and drinks, we ran into Cameron. "Where are you all sitting?" he asked.

"We're in special seats," I responded.

"Have you thought about what I said?" he asked. I'm sure Cecil heard him. It wasn't like Cameron was trying to talk low so he couldn't.

"I thought about it. I'll let you know later."

"Cool. Cecil, man, what's up?" Cameron said as an afterthought.

On the way up the stands, I asked, "Why do you put up with his cockiness?"

"Because I know that's all he has. See, me, I have more to offer so there's no need for me to be cocky." He led the way up the stairs. I liked his response. Cecil wasn't cocky, but he sure was confident.

"You probably thought we weren't coming back," I said, as we took our seats next to Britney.

"I thought I was going to have to knock out one of the cheerleaders for her drink," Britney said as she faked a cough.

Cecil and I laughed. The game was close. We ended up winning by a touchdown. We cheered right along with the rest of the crowd on our side. The home team people were sadly disappointed. I hadn't heard that many boos since I watched an episode of Showtime at the Apollo.

"I forgot to ask you how you got here," I said.

Cecil responded, "My brother let me use his car. If you like I can give you and Britney a ride home."

Britney interrupted, "My mom's picking us up from the school so I better ride the bus."

I looked at Britney as I tried to decide on what I wanted to do. Britney made the decision for me. "Go ahead and ride with Cecil. If anything happens to you, I know exactly who to come looking for."

"Oh, she's in good hands with me," Cecil responded and I believed him.

~ 42 ~
He's Mad

"I had no idea you lived over in the big houses," Cecil said, as he drove through my neighborhood.

"Been here for the last ten years but we might be moving," I said, sounding a little sad.

"Where to? I can't imagine anyone wanting to move from over here," he responded.

"I don't feel like talking about it right now," I responded.

"I didn't mean to make you feel bad. Know that you can always talk to me. We're going to always be friends remember," Cecil said.

"We're almost at my house. Turn left and the

house is to the right. You can pull up in the drive-way."

I watched Cecil's mouth drop open. "This is a mansion. No wonder you're not sure you want to talk to me."

Everyone was usually impressed when they first saw our house. I took a mental picture of the house from the outside because I never knew when my dad would come in and announce we were moving.

Cecil pulled up in the driveway. Being the gentle-man that he was, he got out and opened my door. I said, "Thanks."

The stars shined brightly above. This was the moment we both had been waiting for as Cecil stood directly in front of me. "Can I get my answer now?" Cecil asked. I swore his voice sounded deeper than before.

We were so close, I'm sure he could hear my heart beat. I responded, "The answer is . . ."

"What is this?" My dad asked, as he opened up the door and the bright light from inside shined on Cecil and I standing in front of his car.

"Dad, this is Cecil. He drove me from the game. I didn't feel like riding the bus." For dramatic purposes, I held my stomach. "Cecil thanks. I'll see you later, but the bathroom is calling me."

"Hi Mr. Sanchez," Cecil said.

"Good night young man," my dad said, as I brushed past him and headed straight to the bathroom.

My stomach wasn't upset but due to the stress of my dad seeing me with a boy, it sure was turning some cartwheels. I pretended to be using the bathroom. When I entered my bedroom, I was surprised to see my dad sitting in the chair and he looked upset.

"Did you really go to the game or were you out messing around with that boy?" he asked.

"No way. We were at the game. You can call and ask Britney."

"I'm asking you. You're too young to be going out with boys."

"I'm fifteen. You said it yourself; you and my mama started dating when you were fourteen."

"No. Fifteen is too young."

"But dad, please. You're taking everything away from me. Can I at least have something?" I yelled.

My dad's face changed from anger to concern in a split second. "Let me think about it. I need to meet him, his family. I need to see who my little girl is interested in. Who knows, I might even like him. I doubt it, but who knows."

I rushed up to my dad and hugged him. "Thank you dad. I won't let you down."

"You better not," he said.

As soon as my dad left, I called Cecil on his cell phone. "Did you get in trouble?" he asked.

"He was mad at first but he calmed down. In fact, he said he wanted to talk to you and meet your parents."

Cecil said, "So does that mean you're giving me a chance?"

I realized at that moment I had never gotten around to answering his question about being his girlfriend. "Yes Cecil. The answer is yes."

He yelled out, "Yessss."

I was happy that he seemed genuinely excited. For the first time in a long time, I felt like my world was on an upward spiral. I needed something good going on in my life. My phone clicked while we were talking. "Cecil, let me take this call, but I'll call you right back."

I clicked over to tell Cameron my decision. "I've decided that you and I wouldn't be right for each other. I'm not having sex until at least college. You've already shown me you can't wait, so you do you and I'll do me. We'll continue to do so separately."

"You're cold blooded," Cameron said. "You think because you lost weight you're all that and a bag of chips don't you?"

I responded, "Not only that, but I'm a can of soda too. I see your real colors coming out now."

"You're the one who made me mad. Leading me on all this semester," he responded.

I was livid. "So it's my fault that you flirted with me but decided to make some other woman your girlfriend."

"She was not my girlfriend. We were just kicking it."

"Well as much as I don't like Lauren; she had no idea y'all were just kicking it. If you asked her, you two were in a full blown relationship."

"It's not my fault she got caught up."

"You're cold. I'm glad I made the right decision."

Cameron started laughing. "I can't believe you chose that buster over me. He's a nerd. He ain't got nothing going on for him but his brain."

"Although it's none of your business, Cecil has more going for him than you do. Then again, you can't see that because you're too full of yourself. On that note, I'm going to bed."

~ 43 ~

The News Continues

Cameron was a sore loser. When I ran into Cecil on Monday, he filled me in on the words that had been exchanged between the two of them. I said, "I'm sorry Cecil. It's my fault. I know you were trying to be cool with him."

"He said some stuff about you and I wasn't going to let him get away with it."

"You could have gotten suspended if y'all got into a fight," I said. I definitely didn't want to be the cause for him to lose his chance of a scholarship because he was fighting. He didn't need that type of thing in his school record.

Britney walked up to us. "Cecil, rumor has it you and Cameron got into a fight."

"It was a war of words. Nothing physical," Cecil responded.

"Dang. Let someone else tell it, you were in a full blown fight in the hallways," Britney said.

We shook our heads. That's how people get in trouble. Someone was always passing around bad information. Every time I saw Cameron, he would frown up his face. If I didn't know better, I would say he and Marcus are related. According to Britney, Marcus was still calling her. She didn't call in harassment charges because she was trying to be nice. Oddly, Jasmine and Cassie hit it off and had been talking. Jasmine assured us over lunch that Cassie was doing just fine.

"Did y'all see that?" Jasmine asked when Marcus passed us.

"He's such a butthole," Britney said.

"He has some mental issues. I'm serious," I said. "Britney maybe you can talk to his parents or something."

"If you ask me, mental issues run in their family. Talking to his parents probably won't do any good," Jasmine said.

Jasmine was probably right. I dropped the subject. The rest of the day went by uneventfully. While waiting on a file to download so I could finish my homework, I surfed the Internet. The headline that Sanchez Franchise files for bankruptcy hit me hard. I clicked on the link. There it was in black and white, a picture of the headquarters that was located in Las Colinas. What appeared to be a recent photo of my dad and some other man was inserted in the middle of the page.

There were quotes from some of the employees, who were now ex-employees. They were upset yet hopeful that the market would turn around. The article stated that my dad was not available when they tried to contact him. If the company filed for bankruptcy today, then it would be only a matter of time before we would be moving. I got up and walked around my room. I had so much stuff. I didn't know where I would begin. The thought of parting with any of it made me sick to the stomach. I rushed out of the room to find my mom.

She was laid out across her bed. When she heard me, she lifted her head. I could tell from her blood-shot eyes that she had been crying. "You heard," she said, as she sat up.

"Yes, why didn't you tell me?" I asked.

"I just found out myself. I am so mad at your dad right now. He's kept all of this from me and we're supposed to be a couple."

She wasn't the only one mad at him. We held each other crying. My dad walked in the room. "Good, you're both here."

We wiped the tears from our eyes. Neither one of us said anything to my dad. We just watched him as he moved to sit on the bed next to my mom. She scooted back on the bed as if she didn't want him to touch her.

"I wanted to tell you. I just didn't know how," he confessed.

"A simple, 'Maria, I'm filing for bankruptcy so don't be surprised if you hear it in the news,' would have sufficed."

He said with a look of despair in his eyes, "I had a team of lawyers who after months of going back and forth thought bankruptcy was the best way to go."

"Are you gambling? Drinking? How did it get to this?" my mom asked.

"It's the economy, baby. It's affecting everybody. Nobody's buying. Nobody's building. I thought we would be able survive this, but the downward spiral lasted too long."

"Kimberly said this is just what happened to Dion and his dealerships. But at least he has the sports announcer job to fall back on. What are you going to fall back on?"

My dad didn't respond. I asked, "So does that mean we're still moving?" The house was my main concern right now.

He ignored my question. He said, "I do have some good news if you two will let me get it out."

My mom responded, "By all means, share the news."

"The bankruptcy doesn't affect our personal holdings, Maria. But because a lot of my funds were tied up in the business, we're not going to be able to afford this house."

I felt like fainting but I didn't. "Which projects are we moving to?" I asked.

"None. We'll still stay in Plano, but just in a smaller house."

Maria said, "Most people move to something bigger and better. You're telling me we're downsizing."

She sounded just as frustrated as I felt. "Ladies, it's not as bad as it seems. I still have a couple of millions in the bank. Until I can think of what direction to take the company in, it'll be enough to tide us over."

"College. What about college? Will I be able to go to college?" I blurted out.

"You and Zion have money put up that can't be touched. When you turn eighteen and then again at twenty-one, you will be well taken care of, so don't worry. You can go to any college you want."

Don't worry. I wanted to scream. *How can I not worry? We were moving. We were losing everything.* I started crying. My dad hugged me and tried to assure me things weren't as bad as they seemed.

"No, they're worse," I yelled and rushed out the room.

I was so mad at my dad right now that I didn't even want to look at him. I called Cecil crying in his ear. After he got me to calm down, I gave him the short version of my dilemma. "I know you're probably like, 'it's no big deal' but to me it is. This has been my home for ten years."

Cecil said, "Sierra you have a bad habit of trying to answer for me. You can't read my mind. Wait and see what I think before thinking for me, okay sweetheart."

I guess he told me. "I'm sorry. It's just all this stress is getting to me."

"Take a few deep breaths. Let me hear you," he said.

I did as instructed. He said, "Now close your

eyes and think of something pleasant. Breath in and out."

This breathing trick was working. My heart rate decreased. My head wasn't pounding anymore. "I do feel more relaxed," I said.

"I'm going to stay on the phone with you until you fall asleep," Cecil said.

"You don't have to," I said.

"I know I don't have to. It's something I want to do," he stated.

"I haven't told Britney or Jasmine yet so please don't say anything."

"It's not like we're the best of friends," Cecil teased.

"I'm so tired but I can't sleep." If I were to be honest, I was having a hard time sleeping long before this situation.

I woke up the next morning with the phone lying next to my ear. I don't recall how long we talked. I actually slept straight through the night. Cecil brought peace into my world that was filled with turmoil.

~ 44 ~

That's What Friends are For

My Monday blues rolled into Tuesday. I was dropped off at school at my normal time. My mind was on the big move as I walked right past Britney and Jasmine without noticing them until Jasmine called out my name. I kept walking.

During homeroom class, they kept taking glances at me. Ms. Hogan probably could tell something was wrong because she didn't even pick on me when I failed to participate in the class discussion.

After class, Britney and Jasmine waited for me outside of the classroom.

"Sierra, what's up?" Jasmine asked.

"Oh hey," I said, as I continued to walk.

Britney walked past me then blocked my path. "What's wrong? Your eyes are red. You look like you've been crying," Britney said.

Before I realized it, the floodgates of tears started again. Jasmine and Britney rushed to my side. In between tears I said, "My dad's filed for bankruptcy and . . . and we have to move."

"Oh, no," Jasmine said. Her hand went straight over her mouth.

My body started shaking as Britney wrapped her arm around me to calm me down. Britney said, "It's going to be alright."

"No, it isn't. Look at me." I pulled away and showed them all the space in the waist of my skirt. "We can't even afford new uniforms for me."

Britney was speechless. Jasmine said, "You have lost a lot of weight. I can give you my allowance so you can get some more uniforms."

Britney said, "And if you need anything else, know that all you have to do is ask."

I responded, "I don't want your charity."

Britney said, "Sierra, we're your friends. We're supposed to have each other's back."

"But . . ." I attempted to say in between the tears.

"We got you," Jasmine said.

The bell rang indicating we had five minutes before we would be tardy to our next class. "I'll be okay. I'll see y'all at lunch time."

I couldn't concentrate in any of my classes. Cecil had sent me a couple of text messages with jokes as an attempt to cheer me up. Although I found some of the jokes funny, it didn't get me out of my solemn mood.

Britney and Jasmine seemed to be in deep conversation but as soon as they saw me, they hushed. I'm sure they were talking about me. I really didn't want their pity. I put a fake smile on my face and took a seat. "Hi," I said.

"We were just talking about what action we need to take with your situation," Britney said.

Jasmine asked, "Did your dad say where you would be moving to?"

"No, just that it wouldn't be the projects."

"I'm sure he still has money. People in business file bankruptcy all of the time," Britney said, as if she had experience in those type of things.

Cecil stopped by the table and I was so glad to

see him. "I think I want to eat with Cecil today," I said.

My friends looked disappointed but I needed to talk to someone other than them at this point. I got my tray and followed Cecil to the corner table where he had been seated. "I can't solve your problems, but I can lend an ear," he said, as he opened up my juice for me.

"Bri and Jas mean well but I don't need their charity," I said.

Cecil asked, "If it was Britney or Jasmine in the same situation, what would you do?"

"I would help them out of course," I responded.

"That's how they feel, so don't be upset with them for wanting to help out a friend."

I pondered that thought as I picked over my food. Cecil had a point. Maybe I was being too hard on them for wanting to help. I finished my lunch or better yet played with my lunch until it was almost time for us to go to class. "I owe you two an apology," I said, as I caught up with them in the hallway.

They looked at each other and then smiled and reached out to hug me. Both said they forgave me.

Jasmine said, "We need an emergency meeting at my house. I sent Brenda a message about your situation. By the time we get out of school, I'm sure she'll have some solutions for us."

"I need to call my mom and let her know before she makes a wasted trip over here," I responded.

Britney said, "You do that. All for one, one for all; never let the other fall is our motto, remember?"

I responded, "Of course I remember. We came up with that in elementary school."

Jasmine said, "And it's not just words. We mean it."

My mom sounded like I did earlier when I got her on the phone. "I'll have Brenda drop me off later."

She said, "That'll give me some time to get myself together. Sierra, we're going to get through this. How? I can't figure that out now, but we will."

"Yes, ma'am," I responded.

Before I could get to my next class, my phone rang. Surprisingly it was my dad. "Hi dear, just calling to check on you."

"I'm okay. About to head to my next class."

"Things will work out. You watch."

"How could they dad when I'm moving from the only home I've really known?"

"It's not as bad as you think. I already have an idea where we'll move. It's smaller, but it's still bigger than most people's houses I assure you of that."

Whatever it was I wanted to say I didn't. Instead I said, "I'm late for class. Can we talk when I get home?"

"Of course. Call me if you need me," my dad said before we disconnected the call.

"There you are," Cecil said.

I jumped. "Man, watch it. You scared me."

"I had to check on my baby. You okay?" he asked.

"If one more person asks me how I feel, I'm going to scream," I responded.

Cecil said, "You have a lot of people who care about you."

So it seemed. "Cecil, I'm going over to Jas' house after school so I'll call you tonight."

"Cool. If I didn't have a tutoring session this evening I could walk you out."

"You told me about it last night. I know I have a

lot of stuff going on, but I do remember things that you tell me."

"Remember this," he said, before leaning down to kiss me on the cheek.

I felt better the second half of my school day. Cecil's kiss on the cheek was the perfect distraction. His gentleness and patience with me during all of this made my heart flutter.

~ 45 ~
No More Tears

Brenda and Jasmine argued all the way to their house. It was typical banter between the two of them. I don't know who started it, but Britney and I had been around them so much we were used to it.

Once we had gotten some snacks and were sitting around the kitchen table, Brenda re-entered the room holding some paper. "I got several articles about your dad's company and the bankruptcy off the Internet," she said.

She handed them to me. I read as much as I could. My mind was on information overload. Brenda asked, "What did your dad actually say when he told you about the bankruptcy?"

I repeated to her what I had told Jasmine and Britney earlier. "He claims it's not going to affect our lives that much but it already has. We're moving into a smaller house."

Brenda said, "Sierra, I talked to my mom and she's talked to your mom. You guys will still be living in Plano, but just a few blocks away."

"The houses are smaller."

"You girls need to get your priorities straight. The houses are smaller but they are still big. Your dad is trying to make his money stretch. With the way the market is, nobody, and I mean nobody, knows when things will start picking back up."

Britney asked, "How can Mr. Jorge keep money for his family when his company has lost money?"

Brenda responded, "I'm no lawyer or accountant so I don't know. According to the news reports however, he is able to do that, so Sierra, your dad wasn't lying to you."

"Zion is going to be devastated. I guess I better have you drop me off because I want to be there when they tell him the news," I said.

"Bri, you ready? I can drop both of y'all off at the same time," Brenda said.

Jasmine said, "Ladies I would go with Brenda to

drop you off but my stomach is turning and I'm sure y'all don't want to experience the aftermath."

I cut her off. "Ugh. Thanks for sparing us."

"Yes, thanks," Britney added.

I felt better upon arriving at home but that soon changed when I saw Zion's tear-stained cheeks. Apparently I was too late. My dad and mom were both trying to console him when I entered the living room. He ran up to me and I embraced him. "We'll be okay," I said, although I wasn't so sure myself anymore.

Zion and I spent the evening playing video games. He let me win a few games and I played more games with him than I normally would. I had homework but couldn't get up enough strength to go do it. Instead I remained glued to the game controller.

My dad entered the den. "Do you mind if I play?" he asked.

I handed him the controller and moved to the other side of the sofa. I watched them play but got bored real quick. On the way to my room, I overheard my mom on the phone. I wasn't sure who she was talking to but she was saying some mean things about my dad. "He lied to me. I don't know if I can forgive him for it."

I guess she forgot the lies she had told about her excessive spending habits. I hoped they worked things out. I really wasn't in the mood to be looking for another stepmother, like Jasmine. Jasmine's ears must have been burning because she called. "Guess what my dad just told me?" Jasmine asked.

"You're getting a new car," I responded.

"I wish. He told me that he's considering marrying the chick he went on the trip with."

"Wait a minute. He just met her," I said.

"Exactly. That's the same point I was trying to make. Brenda is mad. My mom, well, put it like this. You know the vase that was sitting near the front door when you left earlier."

"Yes."

Jasmine responded, "It's in a thousand pieces. She smashed that sucker against the door."

"Man. So do you think they were seeing each other when he was with your mom?"

"No, that was someone else."

Jasmine's problems took the limelight off mine for a short period of time. I fell asleep but didn't sleep well. Cecil always said I could call him anytime. I was at the point of calling when I finally felt myself getting sleepy. I woke up four hours later.

"Can I call in sick?" I asked my mom when she woke me up the next morning.

"We should keep our regular routine as much as we can."

I sluggishly got out of the bed. "When do we start packing?"

"We need to find a house first."

"I heard you already did," I said. I hadn't meant to let that slip.

She acted like she didn't hear me and kept on talking. "I want it to be in the Plano school district. The house we're thinking about getting is smaller but it's still big enough for our family."

"If you say so," I responded.

"This move isn't going to be easy. We have years of memories in between these walls but as Jorge has stressed to me, the move just gives us a new opportunity to make new memories."

I knew she meant well. I could either go with the flow or be miserable. Right now I would wallow in misery.

~ 46 ~

A Change of Scenery

Cecil, Britney, and Jasmine went out of their way during the next week to cheer me up. I pretended that all was well. None of them understood the pain I was going through. On top of that, the dizzy spells were getting worse and worse. I didn't know how much longer I could hide them from others. Once I lost ten more pounds, I swore to myself that I would stop taking the diet pills.

"So how are things with you and your boyfriend?" Cameron asked, one day when I ran into him in the hallway.

"Things are just fine," I responded. "How are things with your girlfriend?" He probably didn't know I heard it through the grapevine him and Lauren were back together.

"I don't have a girlfriend. I was waiting on you to come to your senses," he lied.

"I think I have the last honest boy because you know you wouldn't be saying that if Lauren was around," I said. Little did he know Lauren was standing right behind him.

"Lauren is not my girlfriend. There I said it. She's just something to pass the time with until you come around."

Lauren used her backpack and practically knocked him down when she hit him upside the back of his head with it. I could hear the backpack make contact. I knew it must have hurt.

"Ouch," he said, as he rubbed his head.

"Oh, so I'm not your girlfriend," she said.

Cameron said, "You heard it all wrong. I was speaking hypothetically."

"You can have him," Lauren said, as she nearly ran away from where we stood.

"Why didn't you tell me she was behind me?" Cameron asked. He was still rubbing his head.

"I was showing you courtesy by not interrupting

you while you talked," I said with a smile on my face.

Cameron tried to turn the situation around. "What would your little boyfriend say if he knew you really wanted me instead of him? I don't think Cecil would like that too much."

"Been there, done that," I said. I was referring to DJ. DJ had tried to ruin my reputation during my freshman year. I was older and stronger so nothing Cameron did or said would be able to harm me in the same way DJ had.

"So you don't care if I tell Cecil some stuff?"

I stood with my arms folded. "Feel free to tell him anything. I know it's not true and Cecil knows. But like I said, you go right ahead. The only person who will be looking like a fool will be you."

Cameron dropped his head. "You're not even worth the headache."

"I'm worth more than you deserve," I said, right before walking away.

I heard him call me a name that rhymed with witch but substitute the "w" with a "b." I responded out loud, "It takes one to know one."

I had Jasmine and Britney laughing during lunch when I repeated the incident with Cameron. Cecil was tutoring someone during his lunch period so I didn't get a chance to tell him about it.

After school Cecil walked me to my mom's car. I told him about Cameron. I had never seen him so mad. "He has one more time to step to you and then I'm going to handle it," he said.

I was thrilled he was jealous but as I stated before, I didn't want Cecil getting into any kind of trouble because of me. He had too much riding on his scholarships and I didn't want to be the cause of him not getting any when the time came because of a mark on his school record.

"He's given up so things are cool. So chill out," I responded.

"That's just disrespectful, not only to me, but to you too. He shouldn't be trying to go behind my back."

Cecil was right. Once we reached the car, he spoke to my mom and held the door open for me. "Talk to you later," I said, as he shut the door.

He waved good-bye. As we were pulling off, my mom said, "I like him. He seems to be a nice guy. I'm glad you listened to me about the bad boys."

"I like Cecil a lot. Maybe once we get settled we can invite him and his parents over," I said.

"That would be good. We'll invite them to our house warming party," she said.

"House warming . . . does that mean we've found a house?" I asked.

"Yes. We found one. I was a little apprehensive about it at first but I think it'll work."

Moving might not be so bad after all. I could invite my friends and also get to meet Cecil's parents. "How many bedrooms does it have?" I asked.

"We've downgraded to five bedrooms. I had to have at least one guest bedroom because you never know when someone will need a place to stay," she said.

"As long as I still have my own room, I'm straight," I said.

"It's actually a little larger than the one you have now."

"Really," I said. My eyes lit up.

I listened to my mom describe the rest of the house. "The yard isn't as big as our current one, but that's okay. I can still plant my flowerbeds."

"So things really aren't as bad as they seemed," I said out loud.

"No dear they're not. We'll have to adjust in our spending habits," she said. "Me, more so than anyone; but I've lived on a budget before so I'll just have to get back accustomed to it."

"If you can do it, then I know I can," I said.

"I thought I would have to join Shopaholics Anonymous for a minute," she said.

"I would have been there as your guilty accomplice." We both laughed.

It was good hearing her laugh. We both had shed enough tears these last few days to last us a while. It looks like moving wasn't going to be so bad after all, at least I hoped it wouldn't.

~ 47 ~

My Little Secret

Later that night I called Britney and Jasmine on the three-way. "Check your email. I have a link to our new house."

I waited for them to pull it up. "Ooh, it looks nice," Britney said.

"It's not as big as your current house but it does look nice," Jasmine said. I expected that type of response from her.

Lately, Jasmine had been a little more subdued. I guess when she realized I was not a threat to her, she stopped tripping. Britney changed the conversation. "Jas, what's that detective's number? I'm tired of playing nice." Britney said. "Marcus has filled up my voice mail box again.

"Change your number," I said.

"I can't. I really don't want my folks to know," she said.

Jasmine said, "If you call the detective your parents will be notified."

"I didn't think about that," Britney said. "I'll see if he stops. I don't want to get banned from using the phone. The phone is my lifeline."

Britney needed to tell her folks. Marcus was out of control. I heard Britney's baby brother and sister in the background crying. I knew it wouldn't be long before she got off the phone. Once she was off, Jasmine said, "I'm so glad things are working out for you, Sierra. We were worried about you."

"Thanks for being there. My dad's going to buy me some more uniforms."

"Christmas is coming up so if you like I can get the uniforms and that'll be your gift."

"Oh, no sister. You're not getting off that easy. I want a real Christmas present," I said.

Before we got off the phone Jasmine stated, "Now that everything else is settled, I want to talk to you about your weight."

"My weight?"

"If you keep losing, you're going to be wearing my size."

"Cool. I wouldn't mind that."

"But you looked fine when you came back after the summer. You don't have to keep losing weight to please others."

"You're the main one who used to ride me about my weight," I said.

"I know and I apologize for that. You were never fat. Thick, but not fat. If you keep losing you're going to lose that booty that boys love."

I hadn't thought about that. My butt was one of my best assets. "Can I tell you a secret? Promise me you won't tell anybody, including Britney."

"You know we're not supposed to keep secrets from each other."

"Now you know I know there have been plenty of times you told Britney stuff but didn't tell me."

"That was different."

"Whatever. Can you keep a secret or not?" I asked.

Jasmine responded, "Yes. Now tell me please."

"I ordered some diet pills and that's helped me lose weight real fast."

"Bren got real sick once taking some diet pills."

"I've experienced some dizziness and slight head-aches but nothing else. I'm fine. Don't tell anybody though because when my mom found out, she was upset and took my bottle. What she didn't know is that I had another bottle."

"Maybe you should stop taking it. Bren says they' not safe and so does your mom. Come on, Sierra. You've lost enough weight, so chill out on the diet pills."

It was easy for Jasmine to say that since she never had a weight issue. While we were talking on the phone, I turned my body from side to side. "I'll think about it," I said.

We got off the phone and then I called Cecil. He sounded sleepy so we didn't stay on the phone for long. He wanted to stay on the line, but I was tired and sleep was calling my name. The next morning I got up and beat my mom and dad downstairs. Lately, I hadn't seen my dad at breakfast or dinner so I was surprised when he walked in behind my mom.

"Maria tells me you're excited about the new house. I was so glad to hear that. I was worried about you."

"Dad, I'm sorry I gave you a hard time about all of this. I just felt like we were losing everything."

"I'm going to attempt to make the transition as smooth as possible. Once we close on the house, we're hiring movers to pack up stuff. Only thing I need for you to do is pack up your personal items you don't want anybody else to touch."

"When do I need to do this?" I asked. I had a football game tonight and I didn't want to miss it.

"We're trying to get everything done so we can be out of here before Thanksgiving."

That was soon. It was already November. Thanksgiving was right around the corner. "I'll tell Jas and Bri."

"Dear, keep it between us for now. I want to get settled in before we start letting everyone know where we're moving to," he said.

Oops too late. I had already showed them the link my mom had given me earlier.

I had a new walk when I got dropped off at school. My smile seemed wider and my eyes seemed brighter. Cecil was the first friendly face I ran into. "You're looking good," he said.

"Why thank you. I feel good too," I responded.

"So what's your secret?" he asked.

I knew my dad told me not to tell anyone but I had already told Britney and Jasmine so telling Cecil my little secret wouldn't hurt. I had his full attention when I told him about our new house.

~ 48 ~

Revenge of the Nerds

"Give me a P. Give me an L," Jasmine and the rest of the cheerleaders screamed as we watched them from the stands.

Britney and I had performed during the half-time show so we were sitting on the sidelines enjoying the game. This was our last game of the season. If we won, we would go to the play-offs, if not; we would be back at home.

I wished Cecil was here, but he wasn't. I waited patiently for Britney to return from the concession stand. My phone vibrated. Cecil sent a text message alerting me to his arrival. I looked around but didn't see him. I finally saw him walking with Britney up the steps.

We hugged each other. Britney cleared her throat. "Will somebody please help me with this food?"

Cecil and I each took a tray. She said, "Thank you."

I said, "Stop hating."

"I sure am hating," Britney responded with a huge smile on her face.

Cecil placed his arms around me as we watched the game. Britney and I chatted during what we considered boring parts. We all sat on the edge of our seats as the fourth quarter came to an end. The game was tied. Our boys had the ball. If they didn't make the touchdown, we would be going into overtime. The timer counted down. I held my breath as the quarterback threw the ball. With only a few seconds to spare, we made a touchdown. Game over. We won. Everyone on our side of the stands cheered. People were jumping up and down. Celebration was in the air.

Britney said, "Hey, I'll meet you at the bus. I need to go to the restroom."

"Okay," I said, barely paying Britney any attention.

Cecil asked, "Do you want me to take you home?"

"You better not. My dad might not like it. I got

him to agree to meet you and your parents later. If we rush it, he'll probably say forget it."

As our conversation ended, we stood near the bus but I didn't see Britney. Jasmine walked up with the other cheerleaders. "Hi Cecil," she said.

"Jasmine," he said.

"I'm cool with you speaking," I tell him once Jasmine is out of earshot and on the bus.

As the bus filled up, there was still no sign of Britney. I dialed Britney's number but didn't get an answer. I attempted to get Jasmine's attention, but she was busy talking to other people on the bus and wouldn't look out the window so I called her on the phone. "Did you see Bri while you were walking to the bus?"

"No. I was wondering where she was."

"We need to go find Bri," I said to Jasmine on the phone.

Cecil said, "Wait up; I'll just drive you to school."

"Jasmine, get your stuff. Cecil will drive us to school," I said.

Jasmine rushed off the bus. "She said she was going to the bathroom."

"Which one is the question," Jasmine said.

My mind was moving fast. "We were seated over

there. The bus was over here. She probably went to the bathroom in that section then," I said.

"I'll wait right here, while y'all check," Cecil said once we got near the girls bathroom.

When we opened the door, we were shocked at what we saw. Britney's frightened face sent a chill down my spine. Marcus had her cornered. He wasn't even aware we were in the bathroom. "Since you won't give it to me, I'm going to take it," he yelled.

Jasmine and I rushed him. "Over our dead bodies."

We started hitting and swinging. Marcus kept trying to protect himself. Cecil rushed in after hearing the commotion. We stepped back as Cecil got Marcus in a headlock. "Britney are you okay?" Cecil asked.

We ran over to her as she slid down the wall. "What happened?" I asked.

"If you . . . if you hadn't come in, he was going to rape me." Tears fell down her face.

Jasmine was on her phone calling the detective that handled her case with the cyber stalker. "The detective is sending someone over right now."

"We need to call your parents," Cecil said, as Marcus tried to remove himself from Cecil's arms.

"This ain't over," Marcus yelled.

"It is for you," Jasmine said, as she walked over and kicked him under the belt.

Marcus bowed down in pain. Britney stood up and walked over to him and slapped him. My face stung from the sound of her slap. "I hate the day I ever met you."

"It didn't have to come to this. I love you," Marcus said, over and over.

"He needs to be committed," I said.

A few minutes later, police officers that probably worked the football game had entered the bathroom. Cecil said, "He tried to attack her."

Britney added, "His exact words were, 'Since you're not going to give it up, I'm going to take it.'"

One of the officers removed his handcuffs. "Young man, you're coming with us."

"They're lying. All of them," he yelled. "I love her and wouldn't harm her at all."

The officer looked at us and then back at Marcus. I said, "Officer, he has left messages on her cell phone. Plenty of them."

He looked at Britney. "Do you still have any of them?"

"Yes. I saved some of them."

"As soon as your parents get here, we'll be able to question you in more detail. In the meantime, I would like for you all to come with me to the office. Now you, young man, are going downtown. Your parents can meet you down there."

A part of me felt bad for Marcus but then again I didn't because he had the nerve to threaten one of my best friends. I don't even want to imagine what would have happened to her if we hadn't shown up when we did.

~ 49 ~

My Super Hero

Britney's father, Mr. Teddy, came down to get us. Once he was secure in knowing that we were safe, he lectured us about the dangers of going places by ourselves.

"Dad, I wasn't even thinking. I was right around the corner from where the bus was located. I didn't even see Marcus at the game."

"Safety in numbers. Remember that."

Britney's mom called while we were being driven home. From her end of the conversation, I could tell her mom must have been crying. When I got home, my mom and dad were waiting for me. "We heard about what happened," they said, as they both held me in a tight hug.

My dad said, "I also heard that your boyfriend helped hold him down until the police could come. He's alright in my book."

I hadn't thought of it. Cecil was my real life hero; although Jasmine and I had put a good whooping on Marcus before he got there. It was Cecil who held him down. I sent him a quick text message after I took my bath and was settled in the bed. He called me instead of responding to the text message.

"Sierra, with everything that happened earlier today, I can't let a night go by without me telling you how much I care about you."

I blushed. "I care about you too."

"No, I don't think you understand. This is more than a crush. It's more than infatuation. For the first time, I know that I'm in love," he said. I could hear the sincerity in his voice.

My heart seemed to skip a beat. "I don't know what to say. I think I'm in love with you too."

"Even if you're not, knowing that you care will suffice."

"I do. I love you too, Cecil," I responded.

We both got quiet on the phone. This was a turning point in our relationship. We hadn't gone out on many dates. We did go to a couple of dances, but we talked every night. I felt like I knew him and I felt comfortable talking to him.

"What do we do now?" I asked.

"I don't know. This is all new to me. Let's just take it one day at a time," Cecil responded.

"It's late. I need to start packing so I guess I'll talk to you tomorrow," I said.

We said our good-byes. I sent a text message to Britney and Jasmine. My phone rang shortly thereafter. They both were screaming in my ear with excitement. "You're the first one of us to really be in love you know," Jasmine said.

"It feels odd. I always thought it would be one of you first," I said.

Britney said, "Our little Sierra is growing up." She sounded just like her mom Destiny.

"I'm glad this night ended on a high note after what happened," Jasmine said.

Jasmine was full of surprises. She amazed me how sometimes she could be selfish but then there were other times when she could show compassion as she had shown me lately. Many have tried to break our bond, but our bond was tighter than ever.

Britney said, "Cecil will always be okay in my book. He was like a super hero."

"I didn't know he had it in him," Jasmine said.

"Neither did I," I admitted.

"What do you think will happen to Marcus?" Britney asked.

Jasmine responded, "They will probably have him see a psychiatrist and possibly do time in juvenile."

"I sure hate it for him," she said.

"Even after what he put you through?" I said.

"Yes. My mom said I have to work on forgiving him. Not for him, but for myself so I can have peace of mind."

I thought about what Britney said as I laid in the bed. I also thought about Cecil's declaration of love. I went to bed smiling. I spent most of the weekend going through my things and packing up some of my more important items. I also decided to donate things that I knew I wouldn't wear or use any more.

"I'm proud of you," my dad said, as he drove me to school the following Monday morning.

"Since we're moving, it was just a perfect time to get rid of some stuff. I still have a lot of new things. I won't miss them."

"Your mom would be proud too," he said.

I wasn't used to my dad driving me to school.

When he pulled up, we saw Cecil waiting nearby. "Tell your young man to come here," my dad said.

Cecil walked slowly to the car after I delivered the message. I stood behind Cecil just in case I needed to intervene in their conversation. My dad said, "I wanted to thank you for protecting the girls Friday night."

"It was nothing. I would do it again if need be."

"Well, that's what I like to hear. Be good. Sierra, your mom will pick you up," he said.

After my dad pulled away, Cecil and I walked towards the front of the school yard. "You know my friends are calling you my super hero."

"Just put an S right here." Cecil used his fingers to outline a big "S" on his chest.

"You're so crazy," I laughed.

"No, crazy is Marcus."

"You got that right," I agreed.

~ 50 ~

The Last Meal

"Will you be at practice today?" I asked Britney.

"I sure will. I'm not going to let the situation with Marcus hinder me from living my life," Britney responded.

"DJ and Marcus are both crazy," I said.

Jasmine asked me, "What if you found out Cecil was related to them?"

"I would drop him so quick, he wouldn't know what happened."

"From now on when I meet a guy, I need to find out who he is related to. First cousins, second cousin, third cousin removed. I need his whole entire pedigree," Jasmine said.

"Cecil has no known mental issues in his family, well at least I don't think he does," I said.

Britney said, "You better check."

They were frightening me. The bell rang. I hoped I wasn't wrong about Cecil. So far he had been the sweetest guy I had ever known. It's not like I knew a lot of guys and anybody would be sweet compared to DJ.

After school, I met Britney for the Dancing Diamonds practice. Without Britney seeing me, I took a couple of diet pills to speed up my metabolism during dance practice. As co-captain, I worked extra hard at getting the team to learn our new routine. Sweat was dripping off my body as we practiced the routine for the tenth time. "This time I think you got it," was the last thing I remembered saying before passing out on the gym floor.

I'm not sure how long I was out but when I woke up, a paramedic was waving something under my nose. Britney sounded frantic. "I called your mom. They are going to meet us at the hospital."

I was a little dazed. "Hospital? What happened?" I asked.

The paramedic said, "Your blood pressure is extremely high so we need to take you to the hospital until we can bring it down."

People were staring and talking as the paramedics wheeled me towards the ambulance. With our teacher's permission, Britney hopped in the back of the ambulance with me so I wouldn't be alone. "Did you get my stuff?" I asked.

"No, but I'll call our teacher and see if she can put our stuff up."

Whatever the paramedics did, it put me to sleep. When I woke up again, I was laying on a hospital bed with several sets of eyes staring back at me. My mom and dad were holding each other's hands. They rushed to my bed side when they saw me try to lift up. My head felt heavy so I lay back down.

The doctor came into the room. "We did some tests. I need to ask Sierra some questions if she's up to it," he said, looking at my dad.

"Sierra, do you feel like talking?" my dad asked.

"Yes," I responded. I was eager to find out how I ended up in the hospital.

"Have you been starving yourself?" he asked.

"No. I eat."

My mom said, "Do you think this has something to do with her rapid weight loss?"

"It could be. We found something foreign in her system. With our initial tests, it looks like you were taking diet pills. Is that the case?"

I was busted. I could lie and say I wasn't but he had evidence, from my own blood. "I was taking them."

"Sierra, I talked to you about not taking those diet pills," my mom said.

"You knew about this and you didn't tell me," my dad said. His face turned beet red.

"I took the pills from her. She assured me she wouldn't take any more."

"Sierra, what were you thinking?" my dad asked. I could see the anguish in his face. "Baby girl we could have lost you." Tears flowed down his face. That was the first time I had seen him cry since my birth mom's funeral.

I felt bad disobeying Maria. I should have listened. Now everybody would know that I only lost the weight because of the pills. I hung my head in shame. The doctor said, "This happens a lot. I've seen too many young girls come through here. Sadly, some don't make it. You're one of the lucky ones young lady."

"Yes, she's blessed and she won't be doing something this silly again now will you?" my mom asked.

"No ma'am."

"We're going to monitor her for another twenty-four hours. Once her blood pressure comes down, she'll be free to go home." He handed them some pamphlets. "This is information on speaking with a counselor. A lot of the young ladies start taking pills and starving themselves because of an obsession."

I wanted to tell him I wasn't obsessed but decided to remain quiet. I hated when folks talked about me as if I wasn't there. My parents were eating up his every word. I hope that didn't mean I would be seeing a psychiatrist like Marcus. I was not crazy.

Once the doctor had left the room, each one of my parents stood on opposite sides of my bed. "Sierra, you were perfect the way you were."

"Dad, you just don't know what kind of pressure I'm under. Everybody around me is paper thin and here I am with an Amazon body."

My mom held my hand. Tears flowed down her cheeks. "This is all my fault. My obsession with weight put you here."

"Don't cry, Mama. I should have listened to you. I should have stopped taking the pills when you took that bottle. I'm sorry I didn't give you all of the pills."

My dad couldn't stand to see both of us crying. "We're going to put this behind us. Both of you need to stop obsessing with your weight. Baby, you're as fine as the day I met you," he said looking at my mom. He then addressed me, "Sierra, you're a beautiful girl. You look just like your mother. Don't let anyone ever tell you any differently."

My mom said, "Jorge is absolutely correct. Men like a little junk in the trunk." They both laughed.

"She's right you know."

"I can't believe you said that," I said. It was rare I saw this side of my dad. He was usually mister serious. Maybe this incident would bring us closer. I used to be jealous of Zion because he got to see his playful side. Now I realized that maybe Britney's mom was correct. Maybe I reminded him so much of my mom, that it was painful for him so he pulled back.

"You have some visitors," one of the nurses came in the room and said.

Britney and Jasmine walked in. Their mothers were behind them. "Wow, you came. Y'all didn't have to," I said.

My parents relayed information to Destiny and Kimberly. While they talked, I told Britney and Jasmine what happened. Britney said, "Girl, I knew you were losing weight too fast. I had no idea you were taking pills though."

Jasmine said, "I told you taking pills was crazy but I'm not going to lecture you. We love you no matter what size you are so promise us you will never ever do something as crazy as this again."

"I guess it's better to be healthy than to lose weight the wrong way and be paper thin," I said.

"You have another visitor," the nurse said.

Cecil walked in carrying a beautiful bouquet of flowers. He greeted everybody and then came to stand next to me. "Are you okay?" he asked.

"I'm fine now that you're here."

EPILOGUE

After the stint in the hospital, I was afraid people at school would find out I had been taking diet pills. No one suspected a thing. They were told it was heat exhaustion. My best friends kept the secret and so did my boyfriend.

This was the day we were supposed to be moving into our new house. Britney and Jasmine showed up prepared to work, but fortunately with the movers my dad hired, we only had to stand around and watch. My friends knew this would be a hard day for me. To have their support meant a lot. We drank our sodas as my mom directed the movers on what to put in what boxes. I didn't envy them at all.

As the movers put the last box in the moving

truck, we walked through the house one last time. "Well y'all this is it," I said.

"Don't look at this as the end, but as a new beginning," Britney said.

Jasmine held up her can of soda to do a cheer and said, "To the future."

Britney and I tapped Jasmine's can with ours. We said in unison, "To the future."

ABOUT THE AUTHOR

Shelia M. Goss is the national best-selling author of the young adult series—*The Lip Gloss Chronicles*. *The Ultimate Test*, *Splitsville*, and *Paper Thin* are the three books in the series. Besides writing books for teens, she writes women's fiction. She's garnered awards and accolades for fiction writing. Be sure to stop by The Lip Gloss Chronicles web site (*www.thelipglosschronicles.com*) and sign up for updates on contests, free excerpts and more.